MARRIED LIFE
and Other
True Adventures

MARRIED LIFE
and Other
True Adventures

Stories
by
Binnie Kirshenbaum

The Crossing Press
Freedom, California 95019

FIC

The following stories have appeared elsewhere:
"Things to Do," *Finding Courage: Writings by Women* (Crossing Press) and *The Beloit Fiction Journal;* "Past Perfect," *Other Voices;* "Evensong," *Playgirl;* "Wheels," *The Albany Review;* "Money Honey," *The New England Review/Bread Loaf Quarterly;* "Full Life of a Different Nature," *The Mid-American Review.*

Cover illustration by Jacqueline Chwast
Cover design by Betsy Bayley
Book design and production by Martha Waters

Printed in the U.S.A.

Library of Congress Cataloging-in-Publication Data

Kirshenbaum, Binnie.
    Married life and other true adventures / by Binnie Kirshenbaum.
        p.   cm.
    ISBN 0-89594-398-0 — ISBN 0-89594-397-2 (pbk.)
    I. Title.
PS3561.I775M37   1990   89-77904
                                                                        CIP

Dedicated to my friend
Ellen

Contents

Things to Do

Mostly I was doing two things:

1. Planning my escape
2. Making lists

The lists were a New Year's resolution to grab hold, to keep my days from slipping by, to organize. A list demands action. You must accomplish before you can scratch off. A fully scratched off list, I thought, would bring me satisfaction. I could sit back and study it, marvelling at how much I'd done.

As lists are very clear and leave no lines to read between, writing out my daily reminders brought to me a revelation: this was not any kind of life. The need to

1

escape it was as transparent as Poland Spring Water, which happened to be the third item on the grocery list. Yes, a list demands action.

The telling list was this one. It was dated January 14th.

Things to Do:
1. Wake up
2. Make coffee
3. Drink coffee/Watch "Geraldo"
4. Make bed
5. Vacuum
6. Dust (if there's time)
7. Call Madeline
8. Grocery shopping
    a. Chicken breasts
    b. Vegetable (broccoli)
    c. Poland Spring Water
    d. Paper towels
9. Pick up Robert's shirts
10. Prepare dinner/Watch "People's Court"
11. Watch "5 O'Clock News"/Wait for Robert

The very chilling fact about this January 14th list was that it was identical to my lists from January 13th, 12th, 11th, and beyond. Oh, there were slight variations. Mostly having to do with the groceries. And with #9. I did not pick up Robert's shirts every day. Some days I dropped them off.

On the 15th of January the list was again a twin, or a quadruplet, or whatever sameness is when you get that high. Except for two things. One was to get my mother a birthday gift.

12. Possible Birthday Gifts
     a. Sweater b. Handbag c. Earrings
     d. Tango lessons

The other addition was #13.

13. Leave

Leave. Make like a tree and leave. That used to be a favorite of mine. Along with make like a banana and split. To leave, I mused, is to bloom, to unfold and sprout wings. To leave like the heroines in the early feminist novels who left and bloomed, but drably. Moths, not butterflies, they found themselves planting zucchini at Plain Jane's Commune for Unkempt Women. This was not how I wanted to go. Better to make like a banana, a snappier way out.

One decision spawned a notebook of lists. Lists do that. They branch off and make new lists the way amoebae reproduce. One reminder, one memory, a doubt each needed a list of its own. I had to be thorough. There could be no rushing out only to find I'd left something behind. That'd kill the exit.

The first thing I needed to know was where to

go. This resulted in two lists: an <u>A</u> list and a <u>B</u> list.

Where to go <u>A</u>:
1. To mother's house
2. Start a Commune for a New Generation of Runaways
    a. Talk Madeline into leaving Henry

I did not like this list for two reasons. One reason was it was too thin. The other reason was it was too ugly. I turned the page and wrote up the B list.

As long as I was going to run off, I ought to run off to someplace terrific. I thought it best to run to the sort of place featured in *National Geographic* or "Lifestyles of the Rich and Famous." For this list, I consulted the Atlas.

The Atlas was in Robert's study on the shelf next to *Gray's Anatomy,* two books which have to do with getting around.

I carried this book of places to the kitchen table and flipped to the index in the back, jotting down the ports of call which struck my fancy.

Where to Go <u>B</u>:
1. Abruzzi
2. Andalusia
3. Arctic
4. Baghdad
5. Babylon

6. Balboa Heights
7. Barren Grounds
8. Belgravia
9. Beverly Hills
10. Black Forest
11. Burma

By the time I got to the C's, I was fully satisfied there was no shortage of hot spots a wife over the wall could go. That was one obstacle I could cross off the list. Some of the obstacles remaining were finding the courage to leave Robert, finding the courage to face the unknown, finding the courage to start fresh, finding the cash.

How Much Cash I Will Need:
1. Plane ticket (one way) . . . . . . $ 600
2. Housing. . . . . $ 2,000
   (incl. gas, electricity, phone)
3. Food (until I land a job) . . . . . $ 500
4. Odds and Ends . . . . $ 500

Although in some books this amount might have been a pittance, to me it was practically 4,000 big, faraway dollars because I didn't have a sou I could call my own. This was because I did not have a job and also because Robert was a throwback.

I used to have a job. It was a job I didn't care for. I did paste-ups for a small advertising agency. This job did not challenge me and was merely a job in this era of careers.

When Robert and I had been dating a solid seven months, I spent one evening whining about the tedium of the paste-up business.

"Quit," Robert had said. "Quit and marry me. After we're married you can take all the time you want to look around for something you like better."

This was why I married Robert. I married Robert so I could quit my job.

Another reason I married Robert was because he was a doctor. I did not have a very good health plan and was afraid to cross the street for fear of being squashed by a car, a squashing which could have resulted in a coma. I had a phobia about going into a coma. I was scared that with my chintzy health plan, they'd pull the plug on me because they'd need my bed. Or my kidneys. They would not disconnect a doctor's wife. I married Robert so I could cross the street in peace.

When I wrote up my list as to all the reasons I married Robert, I saw I was a whore. I married him to be taken care of. Loving him was not on the list but complete dental coverage was.

Once I asked Robert why he married me, assuming he, too, had his reasons. "Because I love you," he'd said. I asked him why he loved me, what about me did he love so much. Robert had to think about that. Finally, he said, "I guess because of how much you love me." To me, that was like one of those algebraic equations which, in the end, cancels itself out.

Reasons Why I Think Robert Married Me:
1. I was there
2. I didn't appear to have much backbone
3. He believed temporary weakness to be a fixed state
4. He believed I loved him
5. He knows nothing about love
6. He thought I could be manipulated
7. While we were dating, I could be manipulated
8. He thought I'd be the sort of wife which was hard to find since Donna Reed went off the air

I might have gotten another job after quitting mine except that the day after we were married, we moved away from the city. Robert had a surprise which he said was for me. This surprise was that he'd wangled himself a position in a suburban hospital where he got to be a big cheese. For a wedding gift, Robert bought me a four-bedroom stone house in this same suburb.

Wedding Gifts I Would Have Preferred:
1. a string of pearls
2. an old shoe

When Robert drove me up to the house in the

new BMW he bought himself as a wedding gift, I said, "Robert, this house is in the middle of nowhere. You know I don't know how to drive. I'll be stranded out here."

Robert promised he would teach me how to drive. He also pointed out that there was a shopping center within walking distance and that the other wives on the block all drove and would be delighted to take me into the center of town whenever I wanted. I had the feeling Robert had cleared this with the other husbands.

Promises Robert Made and Broke:
1. Teaching me how to drive
2. Spending more time with me and less at the hospital
3. Travelling
4. To add my name to the checking account
5. Making love to me more often
6. His marriage vows in general and specifics

If Robert and I had had a joint checking account I would have cleaned it out in a minute. This was no time to be scrupulous. But after agreeing to have my name put on the blue pinstripe checks, Robert changed his mind. "We don't need a joint account," he said. "I pay all the bills and give you money for everything you need."

"These are modern times," I said. "It's anachronistic that I have to ask my husband for money. I should have money of my own."

"Then why don't you earn some?" Robert got a perverse bang out of cruelty stemming from situations he controlled.

A few nights later when he was feeling more kindly towards me out of guilt because he was again watching "Nightline" as opposed to making love, I brought up the subject once more. "Robert," I said, "I'd really feel better if I had money at my disposal."

"What do you want that I don't buy for you?" Robert asked.

Madeline frequently said Robert was as good as gold, to which I always said, "Too bad I can't trade him in for cash."

Madeline thought this was a joke I was making. She'd throw up her hands and say, "Oh, you're so bad," as if I were a child who'd made a cute sort of mess like getting into Mommy's cosmetics and emerging with lipstick on my eyelids. Madeline lived next door and was absent from school the year we learned about women being all they can be. Madeline thought we, she and I, had it made. Especially me. Madeline claimed to be green with envy over how much clothes and jewelry and appliances Robert bought me. Appliances I refused to learn how to use. "I wish Henry were half as good to me as Robert is to you," Madeline eyed my ten-speed coffee bean grinder. Henry was in banking and talked to me once about commodities as if he thought I were one.

"So," Robert said, "what is it you want?"

"Freedom," I told him. "I want money of my own for freedom. For spontaneity. Suppose," I explained in a way which had nothing to do with the facts, "I want to buy you a present. I don't feel right asking you for cash to buy you your own gift."

"You're very sweet," Robert kissed the top of my head.

Out of biology, I lifted my face and planted my lips on his mouth. My tongue made an attempt to probe when Robert pulled back. "I'm exhausted, hon," he said. "I put in a long day."

Other Excuses Robert Has Dealt Me:
1. I didn't spend my day sitting on the couch watching soap operas, you know.
2. My stomach is bothering me. Was that fish you made fresh? Or did you buy frozen fish again?
3. I've got some things on my mind.
4. I've got a rash. Nothing serious. Just an ingrown hair but it's irritating as hell.
5. Maybe in the morning.

There was a spot warm for #5 on the list of broken promises.

When we were first married Robert was after me to have a baby. "I think it's time we started a family," he said.

And I said, "Oh, you do?"

We did not have a baby because I was popping Ortho-Novum. Robert had no idea I was on the pill. I did not tell him and he did not think to ask. This particular escape hatch I kept in its ivory plastic container in my drawer under the stack of Hermes scarves.

Robert thought I did not conceive because I was a flop, a woman with parts missing. "I think you ought to come to the hospital and find out what's wrong," he said.

"Maybe it's you," I said. "Maybe you're shooting blanks." Completely, I relished the minute of doubt which flickered in his eyes before he got hold of himself. "Don't be foolish," he said.

That was the day Robert, by most standards, quit making love to me. I imagined he had his reasons.

Robert's Reasons for Withholding:
1. Why bother if I couldn't produce Robert Junior
2. Why waste it on a woman who once, even if it was just for a minute, questioned his potency
3. He might have sensed I wasn't always interested

Even though it had become statistically unlikely that I would get pregnant, I swallowed my pill daily anyway. I needed to play it very, very safe if I were going to fly the coop.

Things Robert Doesn't Know About Me:
1. That I was, and am, on the pill
2. That I am capable of deceit
3. That I plan to fly the coop
4. That I am skimming money off the top
   and socking it away
5. That I know about his lunch date
   on the sly

One point in Robert's favor was that, despite his
unwillingness to grant me my own source of funds, he
did not pinch pennies or keep tabs on household expen-
ditures. When I, for example, upped the price of his
laundry ten dollars a week, Robert assumed it was
inflation all over. Nor did it ever dawn on him to
wonder why my sweaters were rinsing out in the sink
when I hit him up for fifteen a week for dry cleaning
these same sweaters.

Another way I accumulated money was to take
twenty dollars a day for groceries and then clip cou-
pons, watch for sales and buy generic staples and day-
old bread. In this manner, I was good for sixty dollars
weekly. Still, even at that rate, it would have taken me
well over a year to raise bond. One more year, added to
the year I'd been married, and I would have been a
tamed elephant.

Tamed elephants filled the vacancy left by the

car squashing. I got this worry from a documentary Robert and I watched one night. This documentary was about the domesticating of elephants in India where they turn wild animals into manservants and house-boys.

After locating a group of elephants, the men doing this dirty deed herded one elephant into a pen. The elephant clearly hated this. She crashed her body against the fence over and over, trying to break it down to free herself. She was giving it her all, so much so that she didn't notice the sneak who'd crawled into the pen with her. This sneak, slithering on his belly, tied the elephant up by the legs; the front legs together and the back legs together so this elephant couldn't move an inch. Elephants cannot hop. This was done at dusk. All through the night the elephant thrashed and trumpeted, calling out against this indignity. The elephant made noises which were painful to listen to. I was rooting for this elephant to break loose and stampede the men to a pulp. Only she was roped together too tightly. These men knew their trade. When the sun came up, in the harsh morning light, the elephant was still. Quiet. She knew something she didn't know in the dark. She knew she'd lost. Her spirit had been broken. The sneak who tied her up in the first place had a word for this which I promptly forgot because it was too pathetic.

When that documentary was over, I was very depressed. Robert laughed and said, "You're so sensitive. I'll bet you used to cry over Lassie."

This could be filed in the list of things Robert doesn't know about me.

Robert's lunch date on the sly was a dermatologist from his hospital. I saw them together at a restaurant in town called Friar Tuck Inn where the waitresses dressed as serving wenches. The place was definitely Robert's speed. Robert and this tootsie sat at a window side table and mooned at each other. Even though that was my husband lunching, talking excitedly with another woman, I found it a delightful episode to watch. Funny, even, like it was a movie. Robert's dermatologist had bad skin.

I watched them long for one another across the salt and pepper every Wednesday when I came into town with Madeline who drove in to have her hair done. Madeline wore her hair in a wash and set style she could not manage on her own. This hairdo allowed me an hour and a half to spy on my husband and his pock-marked babe.

It was a small step in the imagination to take them from the Friar Tuck Inn and place them in a linen closet at the hospital where I pictured them tugging at their hospital whites, panting. It was a picture which made me feel safe. A wronged wife has every right to walk out. It wasn't enough that his sort of ways didn't turn out to be mine. So, I stretched Robert's lunches into tawdry affairs so I could get out from under.

I wrote out many farewell notes for practice drills. I equated a farewell note with a deathbed scene.

14

I wanted something poignant and powerful. Yet, lovely in its way.

A Sampling of Farewell Notes:
1. I know about your lunch dates. I cannot stay married to an adulterer.
2. As you can see, I have left you. Good-bye, Robert.
3. I hate you, Robert. I do believe I've always hated you.
4. I only married you so they wouldn't swipe my kidneys.
5. You were breaking my spirit. In another lifetime, you were the sneak with the rope.
6. It wasn't just you. I had to leave. All of it.

When I asked Robert for $250 to take a painting class at the Community Center he said, "That sounds good. I'm glad to see you're taking an interest in something. It's important to have hobbies." Often I expected Robert to introduce me as "the little woman."

Robert got out his Mont Blanc and wanted to know who to make the check out to. "The Community Center or the teacher?" he asked.

"I'm not sure," I said. This fit right in with Robert's ideas of my being a bubblehead, ignorant of the ways of the world. "Why don't you just make it out to 'Cash' to be safe," I suggested.

Robert wasn't keen on that. He thought I might lose the check between home and the Community Center, which was four blocks away. "Then anyone who found it could cash it," he said. As if I didn't know this.

I asked myself what was I thinking when I married Robert.

Thoughts on My Wedding Day:
1. There's still time to back out
2. I must be out of my mind
3. People can change
4. No one could really be that smug. I can break him of that habit.
5. There's always divorce
6. I really hated that job
7. Nothing. I wasn't thinking anything.

I told Robert not to worry over my losing the check. "I'll put it in my sock for safekeeping."

The next morning I took the check to the bank where the teller asked to see my driver's license. "I don't have one," I said.

"Some other form of I.D. then?" she asked.

I did not have any I.D. with me. As far as the bank was concerned I either did not exist or was a petty criminal. "I'm the man's wife," I said. "That is my husband's check."

That fool of a teller wanted to call Robert up for

verification of this. "It's for your own protection," she said.

"I don't need any protection," I told her. "I need the money." I took the check back.

In the middle of the night I woke up feeling like I couldn't breathe. I'd had another one of those dreams. Next to me, Robert was sleeping soundly. I watched his chest rise and fall with regular inhales and exhales. This made me so mad I slapped him hard. Good reflexes had me feigning sleep as Robert sat up with a start. "Who? What?" he said. "Hey," he shook me. "You just slapped me."

"I did? Are you sure?" I asked. "I was sleeping. I guess I was having a bad dream. Sorry." I turned over, leaving Robert to nurse the side of his face.

Dreams I Have A Lot:
1. I am trapped in a box
2. I am trapped in a box under water
3. Robert is choking me
4. Robert is choking me in a box under water
5. I'm locked in a broom closet with no way out
6. I'm locked in a broom closet with an elephant

It wasn't just the bad dream which made breathing difficult. I'd picked up one of those whopping cases of the flu, some out-of-town variety which battered my bones and bruised my internal organs. I ached every-

17

where and ran a fever I was certain was going to leave me brain damaged. I'd never been sick with Robert before so I asked him to phone my mother or Madeline because I wanted sympathy and not some clinician with a chart. I wanted someone to hold my hand and mop my brow and feed me soup. "I can do that," Robert said. And sure enough, he did.

In the delirium of fever I wrote a list, a list as to why I should not run off.

Reasons To Stay:
1. Robert takes care of me when I'm sick
2. Robert takes care of me when I'm not sick
3. Robert pays all the bills
4. I never have anything to worry about
5. I don't even know what's out there
6. As long as I'm here, I'm not afraid of dying
7. I haven't had a job in over a year

When my fever broke I reread this list which I kept intact except for the heading. I changed that to read: Reasons To Leave.

As the painting class ruse proved to be a bust, I needed to come up with alternative plans for cash.

Other Ways To Get Money:
1. Borrow from mother
2. Borrow from Madeline
3. Hock jewelry

Borrowing from my mother was chock full of obvious pitfalls. My mother was the stoic sort who thought happiness was akin to beauty; not everyone gets it so you take what you do have and use mascara.

I called Madeline on the phone and asked her if she had any money I could borrow. "Hang on," she said, "I'll look." Madeline came back and said she had seventeen dollars. "There's probably some loose change under the couch pillows I could dig out. Will that be enough?"

"No," I said. "I need more like a thousand."

"Uh oh," said Madeline. She thought I was pregnant and after a high-priced abortion. "Are you sure you want to do this? Have you discussed this with Robert?"

I told Madeline why I really wanted the money because that was easier than making something up. Madeline said I was out of my mind. "Give me one good reason to leave Robert," she said.

So I did. "Last night," I told her, "I bought two chocolate eclairs. From that new French bakery. After dinner I was doing the dishes and Robert wanted to know what was for dessert. So I told him there were two chocolate eclairs on the top shelf of the refrigerator. I did not think I had to tell him one of those eclairs was for me. He ate both of them, Madeline. Without even asking me if I wanted so much as a bite."

Madeline thought I was making too much of this. "Come on," she said. "A chocolate eclair. You'd

19

leave Robert over a chocolate eclair?"

"There's more," I said.

"Like what?" Madeline asked.

Things I Never Told Anyone About Robert:
1. The eclairs were not an isolated incident. Robert always eats both desserts.
2. Whenever I offer an opinion, Robert chuckles softly to himself.
3. In the past four months Robert has made love to me less than six times.
4. Robert lunches with a dermatologist who has bad skin.
5. Before we were married Robert gave me a dose of the clap.

In light of the fact that he was, after all, a doctor, I found it quasi-unforgivable that he infected me with venereal disease. He should have known what was what.

Rather than apologize, which aside from the penicillin was all I was really after, Robert adopted the role of the accuser. "In my considered opinion," he said, "it was you who gave it to me."

This wasn't, but should have been, on the list of things I was thinking on my wedding day.

While Madeline was getting her weekly wash and set, instead of peering into the Friar Tuck Inn, I went to the local jewelry store. I had a treasure chest of necklaces and bracelets from this gyp joint; enough factory-produced ropes of gold to hang myself from. This jeweler, being the only game in town, cleaned up on husbands trying to buy clear consciences with 14Kt. gold beads.

Before going inside, I took off my engagement ring and wedding band. They made no effort to stay on my finger and slid off like they'd been greased.

The jeweler offered me $800 for the duo. This was a lousy price and I told him so. He shrugged. "I don't deal in this sort of thing. My customers are already married. All I can do with these items is melt down the gold and reset the diamond."

"Melt down the gold?" I asked. "So these rings won't even exist?"

"That's right," he said.

I grabbed up the $800 and left the tokens of my marriage with this man who was going to melt them away. My wedding band might reincarnate as "Marcy" or "Sheila," a gold nameplate hanging from a thin chain.

Even though my passport had years left until it expired, I wanted a new one, one that didn't bear the stamp from an island in the Caribbean under French domain. Robert and I spent a long weekend there which was supposed to be a full week. We cut it short because we were bored. "I'm going out of my skull," Robert had said. "How many hours can you spend sitting by a pool without going out of your skull?"

"We could do something else," I offered.

"Like what?" Robert wanted to know. "Not the beach." Robert did not like sand. It got everywhere.

"We could go into town. It's supposed to be charming."

"These towns aren't safe," Robert said. "As a matter of fact, they are downright dangerous."

I wanted my new passport to bear my old name and newer looking me on the picture. I wanted to be rid of Robert's judgements as my mirror, reflecting the way I dress, wear my hair and speak my piece.

How I Am Up Front:
1. Shoulder-length blonde hair worn loose
2. Never wear heels more than one inch (Robert is barely taller than me)
3. Very light make-up
4. Good, but not ostentatious, jewelry
5. Good conversationalist but don't go too deep
6. About as informed as the "5 O'Clock News" allows
7. A nice person although inclined to snap nonsensically

At Hair Fare, I found Madeline under the dryer reading last month's fashion magazines. She lifted the plastic helmet off her head and asked me what I was doing here. We were supposed to meet at The Teapot in a half an hour.

"I'm going to get a make-over," I told her.

The stylist tied a pink bib around me and asked if I had anything special in mind.

"Real short," I said.

"Are you sure?" She combed out my tangles. "Every time I cut long hair to short, they always cry on me. I don't want anyone crying on me."

"Real short," I repeated. "Like his," I pointed to the man who was feeling Madeline's curlers for dampness.

I had no idea my hair had weighed so much. I felt light, unburdened, the way I feel after a long day of shopping to come home and put the packages down. What was left of my hair, I had dyed black.

"Your blonde hair." Madeline was the one who cried. "Your beautiful, long blonde hair. Did you save it, at least?"

Other Ways to Change My Appearance:
1. Wear three-inch heels
2. A bold red lipstick
3. Jingle-jangly costume jewelry such as earrings which are fruit bowls
4. Own up to what I think
5. Remove tail from between legs
6. Eyeliner (maybe)

I was going to claim, when Robert asked why I

wasn't wearing my wedding rings, that I took them off because they pinched. In its way, this was true, but Robert never asked. I gathered he did not notice, having gotten caught up with the fact that he didn't take to my haircut any better than Madeline. Hideous was the word he used. "What's with you?" he asked. "Don't you have anything better to do with your time?" I suspected he was after me to dust more.

Robert had an allergy to dust. I rather liked the stuff especially when it grew to be dustballs. Dustballs reminded me of mini-tumbleweeds when they rolled out from under the couch. Robert picked one up between his thumb and index finger and dropped it in the trash. While washing his hands off from this adventure he said, "Maybe you can wear a wig."

The day my new passport arrived Robert wanted to know what the Atlas was doing in the kitchen.

"I was looking up places to go," I said.

"I told you, hon," Robert put on his apologetic voice, "I don't think I'll have time for a vacation this year."

"Maybe I'll go alone," I said.

Robert chuckled softly to himself.

I had $4,063. I counted it three times and then called Madeline. I told her to come right over. I took her into my bedroom and opened the closets and dresser drawers. "Take whatever you want," I said.

Madeline looked at me like I was a cross between the Good Fairy and a March hare. She wasn't sure if she were awake or not. "I'm serious," I said. "Take whatever you want. Take it all."

While Madeline was grabbing up cashmere sweaters and Hermes scarves, I told her my side of things because I wanted to tell someone. "It's just not what I wanted," I said. "I didn't know what I was doing and I tried this and now I know what I don't want. That's something. It's enough to go on."

Madeline wanted to know how I thought she'd look in the bottle green chiffon I wore last New Year's Eve. "With my coloring, I don't know," she held the dress next to her cheek.

I left Madeline in the bedroom to pick over her loot. I sat down at the kitchen table and wrote up a list.

Things To Do:
1. Drop off Robert's shirts
2. Lose laundry ticket on way home
3. Pack a light suitcase
4. Passport and money in inside pocket-book flap
5. Write farewell note
6. Staple farewell note to lampshade
7. Call for taxi
8. Gather courage
9. Gather suitcase
10. Make like a banana and leave.

Past Perfect

for Peter

I am busy trying to spear a creamed scallop with my fork when Harry mentions that a man at the next table is staring at me. "And I do mean staring," Harry says.

"Where?" My fruit du mer falls to the floor. "Which one?"

Harry indicates with a nod and instructs, "Don't you gawk, too."

I want to know why not. "If he can stare at me, surely I can stare back at him."

Harry and I are lunching at La Fortune on Madison Avenue. Harry is treating me to lunch because Harry always treats me to lunch. And dinner. And anything else we might do. This is because I believe in

27

being equitable. Harry makes a pile of money and I don't.

La Fortune is Harry's pick, a babe of a place dating back to a mere 1967. To my way of thinking, 1967 was practically this morning. I prefer buildings to be pre-war; old enough to have witnessed things. This place reminds me of those A-frame houses that get slapped up in an hour's time. Pine wood walls not sturdy enough to contain the ages.

Harry has something he wants to talk with me about. Late last night he called me up and said he had to talk to me and I said, "Shoot," but Harry didn't want to talk on the phone even though I assured him the lines were not tapped.

"Can't I come over?" Harry asked.

Next to me in bed, my Stork Club ashtray balanced on his chest, someone named Kipper was blowing imperfect smoke rings. "I've got company," I said.

"Oh," said Harry. "I see."

"How about lunch tomorrow?" I asked.

Harry said that was fine. "La Fortune at one," and he hung up.

Only now Harry is taking his sweet time getting to his point which I don't much mind, if at all, as I'm finding the business with the man at the next table a fetching diversion. "Why do you think he's staring at me so?" I ask Harry.

"I have no idea," Harry says. "He's looking like

he knows you from some place. Do you know him or not?" Harry's annoyance holds a sliver of hysteria. Harry hates intrigue and bad etiquette especially in restaurants where the maitre d' knows him by name.

"I don't think I know him," I say, "but I might not object to an introduction."

Harry groans, and as if his resignation to fate were a mating call of sorts, the man excuses himself from his table and comes over to ours. "Well, well, well. Imagine running into you here," he says to me.

"And how lovely to see you again," I say. Although there's something familiar about him, I really don't have a notion as to who he is. I press to attach a place or a date to his face but come up empty.

With a wedding-banded hand, the man slips a business card next to my plate. I glance at it. A. Ralston Stoddard. Consultant. I am not able to pin down the name either. He tells me to call him. "At the office," he adds. "We can have lunch. Or something."

"So," asks Harry, "who is he?"

I shrug and pass along the business card. Harry reads it and says, "Ralston? Any relation to the puppy chow people?"

"I don't know," I say. "It's all a mystery to me."

"How is it," Harry wants to know, "everywhere we go we run into old boyfriends of yours?"

I tell Harry that A. Ralston Stoddard isn't an old boyfriend despite the smarmy look he gave me.

"Someday," Harry warns, "your past is going to

catch up with you."

"Don't be silly, Harry. The past can't catch up with anyone. It's the past. It would have to break some law of physics to do that. And now, if you'll excuse me for a moment, I'd like to go fix my face."

While I reapply my lipstick I think about the millions upon millions of people in the Soviet Union who are, right at this moment, wandering around asking, "So who exactly was this Stalin fellow anyway?"

What Harry cannot seem to grasp is that history, once you have one, spreads its legs wide open for selectivity and revision. The beauty of the past is its flexibility to suit all occasions. In that regard, it's like your basic black dress. Sometimes, it needs a string of pearls but you can also wear it with combat boots.

Even the Germans, with all their acclaim as the definitive bad guys, pulled it off by taping cardboard strips over any mention of what's his name in all library books. Then, they took offense over not being asked to the celebrations hosted by the French commemorating the 40th anniversary of the liberation at Normandy. "Are we not part of NATO? Are we not one of the Allied Nations?" The Germans behaved as if it were Brigitte Bardot's birthday party they'd been excluded from. They rewrote their past so they didn't have any part in it. Or at least not any major role.

Harry ought to try asking a Frenchman about Vichy and find out the only Vichy the French are willing to identify is bottled water. I have to wonder if

Harry realizes that the outstanding reputation the French maintain as romantics has a whole lot more to do with burning Joan of Arc and beheading Marie Antoinette than any stroll along the Seine or Charles Boyer accent.

I return to the table as Harry is slipping his wallet into his jacket pocket. He stands for me as I take my seat. Harry has nice manners. He's a tax man.

"We didn't get a chance to talk," Harry says. "I really wanted to talk with you about something."

What I assume Harry's got on his mind is investments. Harry is always after me to open a CD or an IRA, calling to tell me about some bank in Amarillo, Texas offering top dollar interest rates. Harry believes I ought to invest for a later date which I find slightly absurd. How could I invest for a time I know nothing about? Harry also thinks I ought to have insurance and often he mails me glossy pamphlets outlining medical and dental plans or detailing what happens to the family when the breadwinner goes out for a pack of cigarettes and gets hit by a bus. Harry is insured to the hilt. If Harry should lose a toe, Prudential has to pay him $1,500. When Harry told me about that, I tried to talk him into slicing off the two end toes. "You don't need them for anything, Harry," I said. "And you know men were always lopping off body parts, ears and whatnot, for girls." But Harry said something about insurance fraud and refused to listen to what we could do with the three grand.

"We can talk later, can't we?" I ask. Harry is

taking me to a party this evening. "There's no real hurry, is there? This isn't like the silver market, is it? Buy now or lose my shirt?"

"No," says Harry. "It isn't like the silver market."

Harry puts me in a cab and gives the driver my address along with a ten dollar bill. When I am certain we are out of Harry's sight, I instruct the driver to turn the cab around and head downtown to the Village.

I have a rendezvous with Daniel and am already late. We are to meet at Montana Eve, an establishment chronologically newer than La Fortune but which has already managed to acquire notoriety. Like Hanover Street in London, it's the place to go when you're up to something. Everyone there is involved in illicit doings, paired off with people they're not supposed to be with. Montana Eve is the city's answer to the motel. Should you happen to spot a familiar face in one of the darkened booths, the code is that of Sergeant Schultz: I see nothing. I know nothing.

Daniel and I meet here because Daniel has got himself a wife. She's the same one he's had for twenty-nine years. Next year, I'll be 29.

My romance with Daniel has had the same history as the League of Nations, a whole lot of hoopla which amounted to nought. Still, we cling to forms of it by way of the United Nations and the Warsaw Pact. Once a month or so, Daniel and I meet and make strong allusions to the past we never did have together. The facts, not the history, were that Daniel and I never did much of anything unless you count a handful of smooches in his office and an occasional grope thrown in for the spirit of the thing. That I was once his student in a seminar entitled "The Glory and the Dream: 1932-1945" is a point we've X'd out altogether. It's a point that does not fit into how we want to remember this affair because it hasn't anything to do with life and death or foxholes or honor.

Yet to hear Daniel and I tell it we've done plenty. We talk as if we go way, way back. We imply we were together in war-torn Czechoslovakia humping away while Nazis storm trooped or whatever it was they now say they didn't do. Daniel always drinks scotch and I have brandy and we both bemoan the fact that absinthe is nowhere to be found. We talk of battles and espionage, of courts and czars, propaganda and of my underwear. When I wear red panties, Daniel is inspired to fill me in on Lenin driving through the Ukraine in his Rolls Royce preaching power to the peasants. My lavender garter belt holding up black stockings reminds Daniel of the bombing of Dresden and a white linen chemise gets me the sorry tale of Anne Boleyn.

Daniel is sitting in the second booth from the rear toying with his scotch on the rocks. He signals to the waitress to bring my brandy and asks me if I am hungry. I wave the question off. Food has no place at our table. Other needs are pressing. After all, did we not know each other in an era where a potato was dinner for two? Besides, I just had that big lunch with Harry.

To the tune of bomber planes circling in our heads, Daniel and I grow hot. He takes my hands across the table. Our fingers lace. Daniel curses the fates which kept us apart. "If only it had been different," he says to me. "A cruel destiny played out like a game of blackjack in a political deck."

And I say, "That damn war changed everything."

Neither of us would dream of mentioning that all that's kept us apart was Daniel's getting married before I got born and a mutual respect for things older than I am. We crave our history more than we could possibly crave one another.

When our drinks are done, I get ready to leave. Already, Daniel is looking like an old sepia newsreel in shades of brown and off-white. Bittersweet. A bientot, my darling. I wave a handkerchief in farewell.

Out on 7th Avenue, I am jolted back into this decade. One thing you can say about gasoline rationing — there weren't any traffic jams back then.

To parties, I always wear black, aiming for that silhouette lurking in a hallway effect or a shadow under a streetlamp. I hint that I've got things to hide.

I choose a black Chanel-type suit from the closet. As I dress, I keep tabs on the hour. Harry is as prompt as Mussolini's trains; a fact I remind him of often although Harry fails to make anything of it. I slip

34

into a pair of high heels, the sort which were meant to clickity-click across those same fascist train stations at the eleventh hour. I paint my lips a deep blood red and dab Calvin Klein's Obsession on my pulse points and down my cleavage. I adjust my hat so that a dreadful secret is whispered, mouthed, from behind the veil.

Fifteen minutes ahead of schedule, Harry knocks. "Who died?" he asks when I open the door.

"Who hasn't?" I say.

Harry explains the reason he is early. "I was hoping for a couple of minutes alone with you so we could talk before we have to rush off." Harry sits on the couch.

I remain standing, looking at Harry's reflection in the mirror beyond my own. "What is it?" I ask.

"Well, let's see," Harry wants to know how to put this when I experience a click as if I'd pressed the button on a viewfinder, snapping a brightly colored photograph into focus. "A. Ralston Stoddard," I say. "He was that boy I gave a blow job to in a stairwell at Yale."

Having given a blow job to a stranger in a stairwell at Yale was one of my favorite things to tell about myself. Sometimes, in the telling, I embellished the incident by making that stairwell a major thoroughfare, "People filed past us by the busload," I'd said, "stepping around us saying pardon me, pardon me, trying not to notice anything." Other times I gave the story a new dimension. I'd pretend I wasn't gassed, that sober I blew a strange boy in a stairwell. That it was something I'd wanted to do and so I did it.

What really happened, as best as we ever know what really happened, was I got tanked on those tricky drinks, the sort that taste like lemonade or a frappe so as you don't know you can't stand up until it's too late and you've already fallen down. Instead of getting sick or passing out, I found myself giving someone a blow job. In an otherwise deserted stairwell. All I knew about this boy was that I did not know him although I do not recall ever having looked up at his face. I do recall, however, worrying about snagging my stockings on the concrete steps.

After that, each time I went to a party at Yale I made a very big to-do looking for him. Not that I expected to, or wanted to, find him but looking for him afforded me opportunity to flit like a hummingbird from boy to boy, tapping them on the shoulders and asking, "Were we ever intimate in a stairwell?" And they would say, "No. Why do you ask?" And then I got to tell why I'd asked.

I wanted to tell that story because I knew if I didn't tell it, someone else would tell it for me. It was that sort of story. And while someone else might have gotten the facts right, the chances were excellent they'd get the mood all wrong. I wanted to preserve the mood of this story because this was an incident I was very attached to. It was the incident which set me up with a past. Having a past is everything. Having a past is far more important than having a future.

Somehow, Harry had never heard about this which I find most odd. I'd thought for sure I'd told everybody. "I would have remembered that," Harry says after I fill him in with a *Reader's Digest* condensed version. "What I don't get," Harry asks, "is what made you suddenly remember? After all, this afternoon his fly was zipped."

"Don't be crude, Harry," I say. "Besides, it happens a lot, that I remember out of nowhere. Why, just two days ago I remembered Paul Stowfield while opening the refrigerator looking for an egg."

"Who's Paul Stowfield?" Harry asks. "I thought we were talking about the puppy chow guy."

"Paul Stowfield," I join Harry on the couch, "was someone I slept with once, which was plenty, back in '81. March of '81. I'd completely forgotten him until I opened the refrigerator looking for this egg and Paul Stowfield popped into my head. Do you think there's a connection?" I don't wait for Harry to answer me. I go on. "Of course, it's no wonder I'd forgotten him. He was just awful. He made this wretched little squeak sound when he came. It was a perverse noise like a small dog makes, a Yorkie or Shih Tzu, when you step on its tail."

"Why are you telling me all this?" Harry asks. "What's it got to do with anything?"

"I don't know that it's got anything to do with anything," I say. "It's just that we were remembering boys I'd forgotten, how boys from my past pop into my head for no reason. You know, I'll be washing my hair or trying on shoes at Ferragamo's and snap! I'll suddenly recall Wallace Burke or Ian Marks and then I'll wonder who else I've forgotten entirely and don't you know it, can't come up with any of the others so I'll think they're all accounted for. Then, maybe a month later I'll be browsing at the Gotham Book Mart and flash on Jamie Riker."

"Just how many men have you been with?" Harry asks.

And I say, "Don't you listen? Isn't that the point of what I just said? It's sketchy. We never know exact numbers. How many men were lost at Little Big Horn? Could Napoleon keep count of the dead at Waterloo?"

"That many, huh?" Harry says under his breath.

"Now," I ask, "what was it you wanted to talk with me about?"

"Nothing," says Harry. "Let's go."

It's not that Harry is a drudge at parties nor is it that I'm not very fond of him but within minutes of arriving at this party, I ditch Harry. For the purposes of a party, Harry and I don't have the right amount of time punched in. I don't know him so long that we actually go back together but we've known each other too long for me to create much of a time before. Harry's version of our chronicles doesn't always gel with mine.

Plus, Harry is after a different sort of good time.

Often, he can be found playing the latest parlor games, running in circles after the moment at hand. Harry has his finger firmly on the pulse of our generation; a generation I gave up on eons ago when we went disco. Disco will never be remembered. Our age knows nothing of heritage and what it takes to achieve one.

Once, at a party very similar to this party, where I was also Harry's date, I met a girl who didn't know who Winston Churchill was. She thought maybe he was a building on the outskirts of London. "Like Westminster Abbey," she said, "only nowhere near as beautiful." Later that night, the same girl cornered me in the bathroom. I had an eyelash stuck in my eye which I was trying to extricate without smudging my mascara while she stood over me talking about indiscretions. She told me I ought to worry about my reputation. "You don't want to encourage gossip," she said.

And I said, "History is merely gossip. Oscar Wilde said that." Then I told her Oscar Wilde was a national park on the outskirts of Frankfurt.

Harry is tossing macadamia nuts in the air and catching them with his mouth when I find the Southern boy. He is leaning against a wall watering a cactus with tequila. He is from Georgia. He tells me this with a pride I'd thought limited to those from the more desirable Manhattan neighborhoods. He tells me about his homeplace where acacia trees grow and Spanish moss haunts swampland. He tells me about the school he went to where the Confederate flag hung in glory and alone until he was in the sixth grade and they were forced to hang a Yankee flag beside it. He tells me it is cold here. I don't know if he tells me his name or not but I take to calling him Beau Regarde for the General and also because he does look pretty.

Beau is telling me about Reconstruction and carpetbaggers when Harry joins us with some girl in tow. Harry wants me to settle an argument they are having. "Do you say," Harry asks, "*gave* or *had given*? I *gave* her the book or I *had given* her the book?"

"Ah, past perfect," I smile at the Southern boy.

"What?" Harry says.

"*Had given* is the past perfect tense."

"So?" Harry asks. "That doesn't answer my question."

"Sure it does," I say.

The girl with Harry pulls at his arm. "Come on," she says. "Let's go ask someone who knows."

I leave the party while Harry is talking oil prices with a man wearing a Rolex. Harry trusts anyone wearing a Rolex because Black Tuesday 1929 isn't a vivid date for Harry. Harry maintains the market is solid. I go home with the boy from Georgia.

Beau Regarde takes me to his apartment which hardly has any furniture in it. I ask him if he's considered buying a chair and he says, "What for? It's not like this is home."

We take off our clothes, piling them into separate heaps (his-hers; North-South) on the floor. Before getting into bed, he puts *Gone With the Wind* on his VCR and fast forwards it to the burning of Atlanta. Several times we watch Atlanta go up in flames. Beau presses into me hard. It would have been meaningless to remind him about Fort Sumter and who fired the first shot. That's got nothing to do with the history he knows. Instead, I say I am sorry.

Beau falls asleep while Scarlett is declaring she will never go hungry again. I wonder if I could stay here always, cooped up with a Southern boy who believes me to be the enemy, in an unfurnished apartment on the Lower East Side. I think maybe I could. I wonder what Harry would say about that. "Why?" is what Harry would say. "Why don't you direct your imagination into something productive and go into advertising? There's a future in advertising."

I don't stay. I creep out of bed, locate my bundle of clothes and dress. I walk down four flights of stairs and flag a cab to take me home.

Harry is sitting on the sidewalk in front of my building. The sun is coming up behind him. "Nice of you to come back," Harry says, kind of sarcastic like I am late for an appointment or something. "Where did you go, anyway?" he asks.

"South," I say.

And Harry says, "You were in New Jersey?"

I tell Harry to come inside, his trousers are getting creased sitting on the sidewalk. "I'll make us some coffee."

I put the water up to boil and set out cups and saucers. Harry picks up his cup and examines it. "It's got a chip in it," he says. "Why don't you buy some new ones?"

I tell Harry I like my cups. Chips and all.

"People talk about you," Harry says.

I tell Harry I know that.

Harry says, "People don't talk about you nicely."

I pour the coffee and ask Harry if he's ever heard of Liechtenstein. "It's a country that has never waged a war, held an inquisition, purged its population or had an empress die while copulating with a horse. And all we ever hear of Liechtenstein, Harry, when we do hear of it, is that it's a very clean country with a lot of banks."

"What's wrong with being clean?" Harry asks.

"There's nothing memorable about it," I tell him. "When you are nice and clean with rosy cheeks and a healthy savings account, maybe someone wants to marry you but you don't get a history. Scandal is at least memorable." I say.

Harry puts down his cup and reaches to take my hand. "I had wanted to . . . "

"Past perfect," I cut Harry off. "That's past perfect, Harry."

The early morning sun fills my kitchen. Harry and I drink our coffee and it's as quiet as the aftermath of the battle at Verdun.

Pravda

"Let's sit a spell," Suzy says. "It's so pretty out. Isn't it pretty? It feels more like spring than . . . what month is this, anyway?"

"November," I tell her. "It's November, Suzy."

"Well, it feels more like spring. Doesn't it feel more like spring?"

I agree that it does and we sit on a bench. Simultaneously, we look up at the four o'clock sky. A deep mauve-colored sky in velveteen. Caressable.

"Did you ever see such a sky?" Suzy remarks. "Demons live behind a sky like that. I expect one to zip it open and come sliding out onto our laps."

"Poets." I turn the left corner of my mouth up in

an affectionate smirk. "Why don't you write an ode to it?"

We laugh because Suzy would never write an ode to a sky. Suzy writes about two things only: Romance and the Soviet Union. This might only be one thing under two subtitles.

"Will we ever," Suzy asks me, "love one boy for always?" This is her way. Suzy switches subjects like she shifts gears when driving. Mid-lane, without warning, and the purpose is to go faster. Given that Suzy can't spend more than a fleeting moment with anything, how could she consider loving one boy, the same boy, for keeps?

We have discussed monogamy often and have more or less concluded it is an ideal. Like Marxism. Only Marxism is purer. Once again, I tell Suzy it may be a possibility for some but not for us. I used to want to believe in it for me but couldn't. Now, I no longer want to. "If we knew all there was to know, when romance makes room for compatibility, how could we help but look elsewhere for what's been lost? Or want to look elsewhere? Which is even worse."

"Eta pravda," Suzy drops phrases in Russian the way other people drop French.

"Which would you rather have?" I ask. "Great passion, though fleeting, or someone to take out the garbage for eternity?"

"That's not any kind of choice. I'll trade you a Camel Light for a Lucky Strike." Suzy offers me an upturned palm.

I hand her a cigarette. She does not return one of hers. Trading cigarettes is ludicrous. All property is shared. Long ago we lost count of who could possibly owe who what. We know Suzy owes me money but we don't know how much. I owe Suzy more than I care to think about.

"You're such a good Communist," she says. "It comes naturally to you. I have to work at it." This is not really so but Suzy prefers to think of herself as spoiled and selfish and I figure, "What's one more delusion?"

Between near perfect smoke rings Suzy wants to know, "What's the trick to keeping passion alive?"

"Obstacles. Barriers. Having but not having," I toss ideas off the top of my head. "Threats of loss constantly hovering about. Do you really think Romeo would've been so hot for Juliet if their families had gotten on like the Flintstones and the Rubbles?"

"Television is so educational," Suzy says.

"Once it's easy, it's as good as dead," I continue.

"So war is good for something, then."

"It looks that way, doesn't it?" We smile knowingly at each other and Suzy notes, "Passion is the gift of the enemy."

"Exactly."

"Hold on. Let me write that down before I forget it." She digs into her bag and fishes out a notebook. While she is writing I think of all the enemies who insisted on becoming friends and ruined it for me.

45

Suzy puts her notebook away and turns to me for guidance. She wants to know if we'll ever be content. She believes I'm psychic, that I know things. For my last birthday she bought me a deck of tarot cards. As I spread them out looking for nothing in particular, Suzy hung over my shoulder demanding the whereabouts of T.S. Eliot's drowned Phoenician sailor. There was no Phoenician sailor.

"You mean he made that up?" Suzy asked.

"No," I told her. "This is an Eastern European deck. The Phoenician sailor is part of the Egyptian deck."

Because there was no way I could've known that, Suzy got spooked and would not hear that I'd only made it up. "Tell me really how you knew?" she asked enough times for me to say, "It just came to me." And we giggled like a pair of schoolgirls over a Ouija board.

I began giving accurate readings with the cards. I don't know how but it was rather uncanny. "Do we believe in this?" Suzy asked. I said I wasn't sure but took to wearing brightly colored shawls and a turban to tickle Suzy's fancy.

It's still not clear if I believe or not. I used to assume the clairvoyance was coincidence but there have been so many of these coincidences, I've come to trust them more and more. Suzy says I must be an old Russian soul because all old Russian souls have more than a bit of the mystic in them.

"Content?" I ask. "Of all things, why would you

want to be content?"

"I don't." Suzy looks surprised. "I was just wondering if I ever would be."

"You haven't been at all content thus far," I say. "So why worry about it?"

"Because you know how I like to worry," Suzy says what's true. She does enjoy a good fret and especially one over nothing.

Two weeks before we'd gone to a professional storefront gypsy. We each paid her twenty dollars but she didn't tell us anything that I already hadn't. Except to tell Suzy she'd never be another Edgar Allen Poe. This made Suzy miserable until I asked, "Who is your favorite poet?"

"Mayakovsky," she said. "Or maybe Eliot."

"Exactly. Not Poe. You can't be another Poe if you're going to be another Mayakovsky."

"Is that what she meant?" Suzy asked. "How do you know?"

"I'm an old Russian soul," I reminded her. "We know."

Suzy and I have been friends for some years. But we do not think of each other as old friends. Old friends are people we don't really like anymore but haven't managed to cut off.

I once lived with a man who said, "Sometimes, I think if you had to choose between me and Suzy, you'd pick Suzy." He stood there waiting for me to say that wasn't so and there he stayed as I left.

"I was thinking," Suzy says, the glint in her eye flashing a devious thought as brashly as Times Square neon, "Michael is so wild about you. All the time he tells me he'd do anything for you. Anything," she repeats for emphasis.

"So?" Michael doesn't interest me.

"So? So, he's engaged. To be married. He's supposed to get married in two months. And you could break it up. Without even trying hard."

"Whatever for?" I want to know.

"Sport," Suzy tells me.

I mull the idea over and then reject it. It's not sport if I don't even have to try hard.

On this afternoon Suzy is in love with three men. One is a translator at the UN. We highly suspect Boris of being a big cheese in the KGB. Boris is sixty years old and says to Suzy, "Ah, Suzanne. What do you want with seventy year old Bolshevik?" Boris is very smart and knows exactly what Suzy wants but the KGB won't let him have it.

The other man Suzy pines for is a dead American poet. She looks for signs of him in the living but is invariably disappointed. So, she has devised a system whereby he visits her at night. "Do you think it's possible?" she asks me. "Or is it my imagination?"

"What's the difference?" I counter and I wonder when it was that I began answering questions with questions like an old Talmudic scholar.

"I suppose there isn't any difference," Suzy

48

says. "But do you think I'm crazy?"

"If you're a crazy person," I point out, "then I'm one too. And what would it matter what a crazy person thought?"

"You're right," Suzy says. "So all I really want to know is if it's possible for him to slip through my window at 2 a.m.?"

"Sure it's possible." I don't doubt the possibility of anything. That's another change I can't recall having taken place. I do remember being a pragmatist, disavowing religion, faith, superstition, hope, anything I could not touch. Other galaxies, infinity, God, were all figments of the imagination or excuses for what we don't know, as legitimate as the tooth fairy. And suddenly, this was no longer so. And I didn't know what to believe so I believed in everything. Or, the possibility of everything, at any rate.

I ask Suzy, "When did it happen? When did you know it wasn't going to be like you thought it would? I must've been eleven or twelve before I discovered it wasn't going to be *Gidget Goes Hawaiian*. I really thought I'd turn sixteen, have a boyfriend named Moondoggie and spend all my time at the beach even though we didn't live anywhere near one. But even after that I still thought I'd grow up, I'd get married . . . "

"To some loving doctor or lawyer," Suzy finishes my thought. Her third love is a young attorney whom not only doesn't she love, she doesn't much like, if at all. She is in the process of trying to convince herself she'd be happy in Great Neck and children aren't so bad if you can afford a nanny. She is failing miserably at convincing anyone of this, but mostly herself.

"Actually," I tell her, "I wanted to marry an architect. And I wanted two adorable and precocious children. I planned on a country club with an indoor pool and my own Mercedes. Everyone I knew wanted these things. They got them, too. How is it I don't want them anymore?"

"Because you never did want them. Don't you see?" Suzy points out for me, "You weren't even willing to share the car. And everyone knows architects are kind of artsy. And I'll bet you pictured those kids having red hair with a volume of Trotsky tucked under their little arms. The seeds were always there. You and I started with the same notions as other girls but slightly off to the left. And you know how leaning to the left can be."

"But when exactly did it happen?"

Suzy is equally baffled. "Do you think it's all some kind of freak accident?" she asks. "Like one afternoon we went slumming and forgot to go home?"

"No," I say, "because then we'd want out. And we don't want out. Because now we'd be lost having things any other way. What would I do with a house, Suzy? And if I had a precocious child, I'd bury it."

"But," Suzy muses, "a rich husband might be nice. If I had a rich husband, we could buy lots of baubles. I could take his money and we could go around the world."

"And what about him?" I ask. "Where would he be while we cruised the Baltic?"

"Who cares? If he's fool enough to marry me, he gets what he deserves."

With that topic temporarily exhausted, Suzy picks a new one. With her next breath she wants to know, "How many men have you slept with?"

"Beats me. I never counted. I wonder if I could?" I think it over and decide if I had a pen and paper and half an hour I could probably come up with all of them. "How about you?" I ask.

"Oh hell," Suzy fans her face with her hand. "I haven't got the faintest idea. I know I passed myself off as a virgin seven times."

"Why would you do that?" One of the conclusions we'd reached some time ago was that promiscuity was divine. Provided we did the choosing. Pity for me, I am never able to like enough men to do it right but I pretend I've been around more than I have.

"I just wanted to see if they'd fall for it," Suzy explains. "And they do. But all of them? I could never recall all of them. I could recall all the ones that were good. And I suppose they're the ones that really count. With most of them, I didn't even have to be there."

"But then we'd only be counting the ones we were in love with. It's only good if we love them. Even if only for the day or the hour."

51

"Then I don't have to include the times I lay there like a sack of potatoes?"

"Yes, you do. They count. For something," I add.

"Forget it, then. There's a good handful whose names I didn't know to begin with." Suzy sticks a finger in her mouth as if trying to remember information she never had in the first place. She takes the finger out, in mock defeat, and asks, "Do you think we're immoral?"

"Amoral," I correct her. Amoral. A description of myself I stole from a boy who claimed to love me. He meant it to be insulting, to disturb me into loving him back, but I took it as a compliment.

"Amoral," Suzy likes it, too. "All the truly great women were amoral, don't you think?"

"That or immoral. Either works."

The sky grows darker. I light two cigarettes and pass one to Suzy. "Thanks," she says. "I owe you one." We titter over that and as the giggles subside Suzy asks, "How is it we understand each other so perfectly and no one else understands us at all?"

"Some people do," I remind her. "Just not a lot of them. Nor completely. Nor for very long. We like it better this way."

"Ya tee lublu." Suzy tells me she loves me several times a day. But never in English.

I always answer, "Me, too," refusing to use those words we've learned are transient. I love you — in English — is the easiest lie to tell.

Suzy sighs audibly. Her small frame heaves as she asks, "Is this a good life?"

"Yeah." I think about this for perhaps the first time. "Yeah, Suzy." I am more sure. "I think it is."

"I'm glad," she says.

"Me, too." I am about to stand up. "We ought to get a move on it," I tell her. "Or we'll be late." I get up and face Suzy. She leans back on the bench as if rising were the furthest thing from her mind and says, "That was a tender moment, wasn't it?"

We laugh at the word "tender" but do not break the spell.

"Come on," I tug at her arm and we walk, somewhat more sure of our direction.

Travail

There to greet me as I got off the train at Bustani were three goats. Dead, stuffed and dressed in pink tutus, these two large goats and one kid were dancing, a pas de trois that would hold for eternity. "Will you get a load of those goats?" I said to Peter. "I can't stay here." I wanted to get back on the train and try another town but, as Peter reminded me, that was impossible. Travel in Roumania was restricted. No train hopping on a whim here. All tickets must be purchased in advance. All the necessary papers shown. And you must buy your tickets for your exact destination. We were in Bustani on the recommendation of the woman in the tourist office in Bucharest. She'd promised charm, mountains, regenerative spas, babbling brooks, a fountain of youth and a cure for all ills. She didn't say anything about stuffed goats.

"We're going to love it here," Peter said. "Look at those mountains."

The Carpathians were black, tall and craggy. On the highest peak on the blackest mountain a cross had been erected. It lorded down at us. I looked away and said, "Well, it can't be any worse than Bucharest." The woman in the Roumanian Tourist office in New York had told us Bucharest was the Paris of the East. She must have been thinking of the Paris of 1942.

The tourist office of Bustani was a block or so from the train station. Peter carried our bags. I moped alongside of him.

This trip to Roumania was supposed to be the romantic venture intended to keep Peter and me together. Our last chance for gas. He had wanted us to go to Italy, carrying on for weeks about the canals in Venice. But I maintained the canals of Venice were sewers. Roumania was my pick. I wished Peter had rubbed my nose in my lousy decision. At least then we could've had a good fight. But Peter didn't do that as he was trying desperately to give us a good time. I hadn't the stomach for his optimism.

Taxidermy must've been the number one native craft in Bustani. A stuffed pelican waved to us from the window of the tourist office. It was wearing a beret. "At least it's not doing the can-can," Peter tried to make it not so bad.

The tourist office was a room with a cafeteria-type table, a telephone and a woman. She looked up at us but didn't greet us or ask if she could be of assistance. "Do you speak any English?" Peter asked her.

"Some," she said.

"We need a hotel room," Peter told her. In Bucharest we were told they could not make reservations for anyplace not in Bucharest. Something about the telephone system being out of order. "But is no problem," the woman had assured us. "Many hotels in Bustani. Beautiful hotels in Bustani."

"There are no hotels here," this one said.

I kicked a suitcase across the room. Peter went to fetch it back. "Listen up," I said. "In Bucharest we were told there'd be no problem getting a hotel room here. I just got off a four hour train ride where our first-class tickets bought us standing room in the toilets. Do not play cute with me. Get me a hotel room."

"There are no hotels here," she repeated, like a defective parrot.

In Bucharest we'd learned about greasing palms. It wasn't like in New York. You don't do it here with money. Roumanian currency had about as much value as Confederate dollars. You had to give the Roumanians blue-jeans or some such thing. I took off my wristwatch and handed it to the bitch. "Now do you have a hotel room?"

"Not your watch," Peter said. Peter'd bought me

that watch for my last birthday but I was too cranky to be sentimental. "You'll get me another one," I said.

The woman came across. She said that maybe she can find us a room. She made a phone call. Yes, there was a room available. She wrote an address on a piece of paper and told us that this must be our luckiest day.

"Not as luckiest as your day has been," I said and we left her admiring her newly adorned wrist.

Two steps out of the tourist office, we were accosted by an old, crooked man who, for the agreed upon sum of three ball point pens, would take us to our hotel. I was foolish enough to think he had a car. Hoisting our suitcases over his humped back, he motioned us to follow behind him. After a kilometer or so, he stopped and gestured that this was the place. The hotel sagged like a mattress slept on for years too long. We gave him the three pens and he jumped around like an excited little monkey. "Peter," I said. "Put a nickel in his cup, would you."

"Come on," Peter said. "Ease up. We got a hotel room, didn't we? And this town is really beautiful. Didn't you notice how beautiful it is?"

"No," I said.

The hotel clerk was asleep behind his desk, and I said, "Maybe he's stuffed, too."

Peter coughed politely and woke the guy up. He showed us to our room and I couldn't help but observe that this place was deserted. I ought to have gone and snatched my watch back.

The whole hotel had a musty smell about it and our room stunk like it hadn't gotten air in eons. "Open a window," I told Peter. "This place smells like a tomb." But the windows were sealed shut.

Peter suggested we take a walk but I didn't want to. "I think I'll stay here. I feel like reading for a while. And maybe I'll take a nap."

"A nap sounds like a good idea," Peter reached out to touch me.

"I'm tired, Peter. Leave me be."

Peter said in that case he would go for a walk. "I'll hunt up a nice place to have dinner," he said. "Sleep well."

I read for a bit and drifted off. When I woke, I was instantly annoyed because without my watch I didn't know what time it was. I hated not knowing what time it was. I threw some water on my face and looked out the window. I was no eagle scout but my guess was that it was late in the afternoon.

I wrote Peter a note that I was also going for a walk. I instructed that he should wait here if he returned before I did. I realized I didn't have a key to lock up but no matter as we barely had anything left worth stealing.

Our hotel was on a narrow side street. Trying to decide in which direction to head off, I looked to my right. Uphill. I turned to my left. A procession was headed my way. Two priests in black vestments were leading a pair of black stallions. The horses were pulling a wagon which was filled with flowers. I stood on tip-toes and saw the body of a man in a casket set in the middle of the floral arrangement. He was covered with cellophane like a plate of sandwiches catered from a deli. The mourners followed the hearse. Heading up this group was the widow. She was veiled. Everyone, even the children, wore black. At the end, lagging behind, were some teenage girls. They were giggling.

When this parade was safely up the hill, I ran back to the room. It seemed like a long time but was probably only a few minutes before Peter came in. "Did you see the funeral?" I asked.

"No," said Peter. "Where was it?"

"Peter, they ride the dead around in an open casket on a wagon. But it's not really open because they cover it in cellophane. Why would they cover the dead with cellophane?"

Peter had some years on me. Twenty of them to be exact. And consequently I always imagined he knew about such matters. Peter shrugged. "It's cheaper than glass, I suppose. And it keeps the flies off the body just as well. I found a place to have dinner," he went on. "Are you hungry?"

I wished I wasn't hungry. But I was. My body continued to betray me. It still wanted to eat. And drink. And sleep. Everything but make love. I hadn't let Peter touch me for five months. He was very patient. And understanding. He loved me very much. I wished he didn't. I wished he gave me an ultimatum: put out or get out. But he didn't. He was waiting for me to come around. It was expected I'd come around on this trip. But it wasn't likely.

"There's only one restaurant in town. As far as I could make out," Peter was telling me as we walked there. "But it seems a decent place."

The streets in Bustani twisted around the mountains. They were narrow and many were cobblestoned. The houses, I was forced to admit, were awfully cute chalet affairs. And each had an abundant flower garden with ducks on the lawn. All in all, it had a *Heidi of the Alps* look. If you didn't look too hard, that is. Because if you looked carefully, you'd notice the ducks were stuffed and the people, plodding along like oxen, had no expressions.

The restaurant was very large. It had royal blue carpeting but no decor. We were the only ones there. "I guess it's a little early for dinner," Peter said. I gave him a look. There wouldn't be anyone here no matter what the hour. We were the only tourists in this town. And Roumanians, we learned, rarely went out to eat. Restaurants there were not special places serving up delectable goodies but rather, only a service provided. There were no menus in Roumanian restaurants. Whatever came in that day via Soviet transport was what was served. The waitress, a brute in white uniform, dropped a basket of sourdough rolls on the table. They landed with a thud. One squeeze told me they were not for eating. "Save one," I told Peter. "Later, when we're bored, we can have a game of squash with it."

Peter waved the waitress over and tried to find out what was for dinner. I reminded him that if it were beef, we didn't want it. The beef in that country had a very bad smell to it.

English, French and Italian failed Peter. The waitress did not catch on. Peter tried hand signals, and he must have gotten through. She went off and returned with a tray. A very large, raw liver was sitting on the plate. For an unknown reason, she saw fit to garnish it with a whole tomato. She stuck the liver under my nose for inspection. "Peter, make her take it away. I'm going to be sick." But this waitress was bent on our approval of the bleeding liver. She refused to budge until Peter furiously bobbed his head with joy. She went, presumably, to throw the liver on the fire.

"Peter, if she brings that liver back, I swear I'll throw up. Can't you make her understand that all we want is some cheese or something?"

Peter got up to try to talk some sense into the waitress. It was a pity we hadn't thought to bring something to bribe her with. But it turned out Peter must have had a pen or some paperclips or something in his pocket for they came back to the table with two salads and one sorry looking baked potato.

Peter was so gallant in letting me have the potato that when he asked, "Maybe tomorrow we'll go mountain climbing," I agreed even though I knew there was no way I'd fad-da-der-ahhl around those hills.

Back in our hotel room, I feigned sleep as Peter rubbed my back. Soon I heard what I wanted. He snored lightly and I relaxed enough to fall asleep as well.

I dreamt we were in this very room. I was face up and the covers were down at my ankles. I was exposed and terrified. Peter was biting me. Not affectionate nibbles; he was like a wild dog with its prey. Taking ferocious bites from my thighs and belly, ripping out large chunks of my flesh with his teeth. Blood dripped all over me as Peter spit my meat to the floor. He came in for another bite. I dreamt he was eating me alive. My heart was beating hard. I woke up. I looked over at Peter. He was sound asleep. I was intact. Sort of.

I got out of bed. Pulling the suitcase down from the closet, I threw my things in, not bothering to fold anything or put bottles and tubes in plastic bags. I hadn't the time for such niceties. Peter woke up. "What are you doing?" he asked.

"I'm getting out of here. I'm getting out of this country."

"You can't go now," he said.

"Yes, I can. You can't stop me. No one can stop me. I'll flee. I'll flee across the border. It's done all the time."

"We're hundreds of kilometers from the border," Peter said. "Better to wait until morning and we can take the train out. We'll take the Orient Express to Italy."

"I can't stay here. I can't stay in this room. I

can't. I can't." I sat on the floor.

Peter got out of bed and sat down next to me. He took my hand. "First thing in the morning. We'll get train tickets. We'll go to Italy."

I shook my head. "I don't want to go to Italy. I hate it here. I hate everything. It's dead, Peter. It's all dead. I want to go home."

"Then we'll go home," Peter said. "There's no point to being here if you're unhappy."

"I thought Roumania would be romantic," I apologized. "It sounds romantic, doesn't it?"

"Sure it does," Peter said. "It's almost the exact same word. Roumania. Romantic."

"But it's not romantic, Peter. It's an awful place. It's all awful."

"So now we know not to come back."

"Peter, why do you have to be so damn decent to me?"

"Because I love you," Peter said.

"I don't love you," I told him.

"I know that," he said.

"I tried."

"I know that, too."

"I used to love you. Really. I used to. Peter? Please hold me and make me not scared."

Peter put his arms around me and whispered about how we'd take the first train back to Bucharest. "And then straight to the airport, no detours," he promised.

I kissed him.

We didn't sleep and so we were packed before the sun came up. We had to pay for a whole week at that dump even though we didn't stay even one full day. Peter said not to argue about it as we had to get rid of the money anyhow. "We can't exchange it regardless. So don't aggravate yourself," he told me.

I carried my own suitcase for the first time since we'd left New York. It wasn't as heavy as it was then. Nearly everything I'd started out with was used to buy train tickets, hotel rooms and access to public bathrooms.

Peter was thoughtful and did not point out that Bustani, with the people still asleep and the mountains shrouded in morning mist, looked as pretty as a picture postcard.

We arrived at the train station and Peter sat me on a bench while he went to the ticket office to secure our passage to Bucharest.

I smoked a Roumanian cigarette which were worse even than the French ones. I tried not to worry that the trains might not be running or that our passports had been stolen or that Bustani was the land of the forgotten. But I worried anyway.

Peter came out waving two tickets. I clapped my hands, ran over to the trio of horned ballerinas and yelled to Peter, "Take a picture of me with the goats."

"I can't," Peter said. "In order to get our tickets I had to give the stationmaster my camera."

Evensong

I answered the phone while lowering the volume on the TV. Sometimes, I'd rather no one knew I watch *Odd Couple* reruns. It was for Stephan. I cupped my hand over the mouthpiece and said, "It's for you. A girl," and turned the volume back up. *The hell with someone I don't know.*

Stephan took the phone. Leaning over me, he snapped off the television. I was about to turn it back on when he gripped my forearm, dug his fingers in. "Stephan," I whined, "that hurts. Let go, will you?" I was damn near bleeding but he ignored me, not loosening his grip one bit, and went on talking to the girl on the phone. "Uh huh. Yep. I love you. I'll see you tomorrow," he said.

He put the receiver back in the cradle and punched the wall. "What is it?" I asked, although I had a feeling I didn't really want to know.

"My mother died," he said.

I'd never seen him cry before except once when we broke up for a while and then I was glad he was crying. This was different. *His mother is dead and what am I supposed to do?*

Everything I thought of saying sounded so cliched; something like "time heals all wounds," but if my mother had just died and someone dished out one of those inane platitudes to me, they'd be dirt in my book. So I didn't say anything.

That's better than laughing, I suppose. When I was thirteen and Rebecca Justice told me her father had died, I laughed. Later, I cried because that was such a crummy thing to do and I figured I had to be a pretty crummy person to laugh over a thing like that. So at least I wasn't laughing this time.

Stephan had his face buried in a pillow while I worried over my role in all this. Stephan's mother was not my all-time favorite person. I wanted to like her. It's just that she didn't like me. Stephan used to tell me she did like me, but I knew better. Maybe it wasn't all that personal, she might have thought I was nice enough, but I think she was afraid of having grandchildren with little horns protruding out from their tuft of wiry hair. *But I never wished her dead. Stephan must know that.*

"Ruthie, why'd she have to die?" He lifted his pink face from the pillow and looked so young and vulnerable. I hate it when people look vulnerable. It makes me want to step all over them. *Don't look that way, Stephan.*

"I don't know," I said, wanting only to watch the *Odd Couple* and pretend this didn't happen.

"Ruthie? Let's go get drunk."

"Anything you want, Stephan." *Good thinking. Let's get very drunk and have a good time and forget all this nonsense about dead mothers.*

We got back when the bars closed, nowhere near as stinking as I would have liked. I was tired. I could barely keep my eyes open but Stephan wanted to talk. "You know what I remember about her most, Ruthie?"

"No, what?"

"I remember coming home for lunch when I was in grammar school and she'd be standing at the stove making soup or something like that, you know. I'd sneak up behind her and squeeze her waist and she'd jump and scream like she didn't know it was me. Like I really scared her. And then she'd laugh and laugh. That's what I remember best."

"That's nice, Stephan. That's a nice thing to remember. Now, why don't you try and get some rest?"

"No. I'm not tired. You sleep though. Ruthie, you don't have . . . Ruthie are you asleep?"

"No." *But I'd like to be.* "What is it?"

"You don't have to come with me tomorrow if

69

you don't want to . . . "

"Well, it's not that I don't want to, but I don't think I should. Your family won't want to be bothered with guests right now."

"You're not a guest. You're part of the family."

The hell I am. Don't ask me to come with you. I wasn't any good with your family under normal circumstances. I'd be a calamity now.

"But Ruthie, would you come to the wake?"

No. I've never seen a dead body before. I wouldn't know what to do at a wake. I'd be sure to do the wrong thing. I might even laugh. You can't want me there.

"Whatever you want, Stephan."

"You're wonderful, Ruthie."

He was mistaken. If he had any idea how I was crapping out on him, he would have thought me many, many things, but wonderful wouldn't have been one of them. I was angry. His mother died and I was pissed off. At what? The inconvenience?

Stephan left early the next morning. I couldn't think of a thing to say while he dressed and packed, and was still mute as he left. I don't know why I couldn't just say I was sorry. *Just because I wasn't best of friends with a person doesn't mean I'm not sorry they're dead, does it?*

I was afraid Stephan was going to remember all the rotten things I'd said about her in the past. Nothing slanderous but snippy little quips like how I thought her inconsiderate because she never thanked me for the cheese wheel I sent last Christmas. Nothing that wasn't true. And I hoped he'd forgotten the fight we had when his mother came for a visit and I wouldn't hang around to say hello. "What for?" I'd said. "So she can talk about the fascinating culture they have in Israel, again?"

I called my mother to tell her what happened and to ask if there was any possible way to get out of going to the wake.

"Ruthie, how can you even think of such a thing? Stephan needs you now."

"But Mother, I cannot look at a dead body. I just can't."

My mother told me I didn't have to view the body but I most definitely had to put in an appearance. This was not an issue up for debate. There was no way out so I asked if I should bring flowers or something.

"No, I'll send flowers and . . . "

"You don't have to do that," I said. "She never even sent me a thank-you note for the cheese wheel."

"I'm going to ignore that, Ruth. I'll send flowers and you send a mass card."

I didn't know what a mass card was but my mother filled me in and told me I could get one at any church. "At the rectory," she said. "And Ruth, try being a little less selfish, now."

"I'm going to the damn wake, aren't I?"

It crossed my mind that getting a mass card from St. Patrick's might have been a nice gesture but Our Lady of Pompeii was more convenient. While poking around for the rectory, I wondered if I'd be nervous talking to a priest. But I never got to find out. There was some kid working there instead. I figured this was the church's way of keeping kids out of trouble because this potential delinquent looked none too thrilled about being there. She'd much rather have been outside smoking cigarettes and checking out boys. "Whad ya want?" she snapped her gum.

"I'd like a mass card, please."

"Two dollas, five or ten?" she asked behind a rather impressive pink bubble.

"What's the difference?"

She rolled her eyeballs as she sucked the bubble back into her mouth. "One costs two dollas, one costs five and one costs ten. Get it?"

"I'll take the ten."

She fiddled around under a counter and pulled out a white, crappy looking vinyl folder trimmed in gold. "Who's it for?"

"My boyfriend's mother."

"Her name. What's her name?"

"Oh. Her name. Margaret Casey."

"Spell."

"I'll write it." I pulled the folder towards me. On the right leaf was this rather ornate parchment expressing sentiments, certainly not my own, in imitation Gothic calligraphy; red, black and green. Okay. I could live with that. But the left side . . . the left side boasted an eight by ten, very purple, very glossy portrait of

72

Jesus. "Are all these cards the same?" I asked. "Maybe I'd prefer the two dollar one."

"They're all the same," she said.

"Oh. You're sure you don't have one a little less fancy? You see, she was a simple woman. She favored plain things."

"I said they're all the same," the girl chewed on her cuticle.

"Oh. Well, here on this part," I pointed to the line where I was supposed to sign my name, "could I just leave that blank? An anonymous donor."

"Why would you wanna do that?"

Because someone in Stephan's family will be sure to ask who sent that hideous thing and another member will be sure to reply, "Stephan's girlfriend. Who else?" But I couldn't very well explain that to this petunia so I signed my name and slid the card back to her. "It goes to Connell's Funeral . . ."

"What are ya giving it to me for?"

"Don't you mail it?"

"No, we don't mail it." This kid had really had it with me. "Ya bring it to the wake. Don't cha know anything?"

"You mean I hand this over personally?"

"Yeah," she dismissed me, pulling a bottle of nail polish from her purse.

At home, I tried pulling out the picture of Jesus but it held fast. So I slid the whole thing into a manila envelope and hoped no one would open it, at least until

73

after I'd gone. I also thought I might try to forget it, leaving it on my desk and not remembering until I was on the train when, shucks, it would be too late, although that beauty wasn't the sort of thing easily forgotten.

There didn't seem to be any point in cooking dinner for myself so I went out for a hamburger where some yahoo at the next table kept making eyes at me while I tried to eat. When I got up to leave, he followed. "Would you please get lost," I said. "I've just had a death in the family and I'm in no mood to make new friends, understand?"

"Hey, wow. I'm really sorry. Is there anything I can do to help?"

There I was trying my damnedest to avoid doing anything and this stranger was offering assistance. *Yeah, you can help. You can tell me how you were able to say you were sorry without giggling or turning red. You didn't choke or stammer. Smoothly and clearly, with a touch of sincerity thrown in to boot, you were able to say you were sorry. How the hell do you do that?* "No, no, you can't do anything. I prefer to be alone."

I wore black. In the movies everyone wears black to funerals, only I was the only one in black at the wake. I arrived at the funeral home early despite my dawdling, lingering and general cool state of heels. I sat in Penn Station, mass card tucked under my arm, drinking burnt coffee as my train pulled out. Hoping beyond reason there wouldn't be another one, I asked when the next train left and was told I had but twenty minutes to wait. *I couldn't miss two trains, could I?*

Any other time that train would have been broken down. Whenever I go to the beach the LIRR always breaks down, but not since Casey Jones did a train make time like this one did. I smelled a conspiracy.

Out on the street, I hailed a cab. The driver told me Connell's Funeral Home was only a half a block down the street. "You can walk it easy, lady," he said.

I got in the cab anyway and asked him to drive around, show me the sights. His eyes squinted like he had some kind of a kook in his cab and so I offered to pay him double to cruise a bit. "I hate to be early for anything," I said.

He drove. I bit my lip. I told myself to loosen up. I told myself that Stephan needed me. I tried to make that matter.

"Okay, lady. We're here."

"Could you drive around a little more?" I asked.

"Aw come on, lady. I can't spend the day going around in circles."

Connell's Funeral Home had five or six parlors with five or six wakes going on at once. I toyed with the idea of going to somebody else's wake. Maybe I'd cast a shadow of doubt on the deceased's good character. That made me giggle and I was mid-yuck when Stephan found me. "Ruthie, there you are."

I halted the chuckles and thrust the mass card at

him as he steered me into parlor number two. "What's this?" He was pulling the card from the envelope.

"Don't," I lunged for it, "open it here. Just drop it somewhere. Preferably where no one will find it."

Stephan was not going to let up until I told him what was in the envelope and I figured I might as well before he opened it and found out for himself. "A mass card," he said. "How sweet of you, Ruth. I'll put it with the others." I couldn't find the words to stop him and this was not the place to wrestle him to the floor for it, so I backed off to a corner, watching him arrange it, spread-eagled, smack in the center of a dozen other mass cards. Only those cards didn't look anything like mine. First of all, they were much smaller. And none of them had gold designs on the cover or flowery script inside. But most obviously, none of them had a purple, glossy picture of Jesus on the left. My card couldn't be missed or overlooked. All the tasteful, white cards gathered around it, gaping. It kept beckoning me to look at it and after a while I thought I saw the Jesus winking at me.

Like covering my eyes and then peeking through my fingers at a horror movie, I stole glances at the coffin. From my safe distance I could not see in it but watched the steady stream of people filing over, kneeling on this little stool and praying. Thank God I didn't have to do that. I'd be sure to kneel the wrong way and all those people would be watching me goof up. And I don't know any prayers.

"Ruth?" Stephan was at my side. "I haven't gone up to the casket yet. I don't want to go up alone." He slipped his hand over mine. My hand was sweaty.

Oh no. No way. Not me, pal. I'm here. Isn't that enough for you? "But Stephan," I said, "I don't know how to kneel the right way."

He told me I didn't have to kneel. "Just hold my hand," was all he asked.

"Stephan," I gave it another go, "I don't know any prayers."

"You don't have to pray," Stephan said, "if you can't."

I would have conjured up another argument had I not noticed a bit of a crowd beginning to gather around my mass card and so I made my getaway in the direction of the casket.

She was yellow; no longer a real person but a statue from some shoddy Asbury Park wax museum. I couldn't look for long and instead studied my feet while Stephan stared hard at her. After what seemed to be a good century, he turned away and said, "Let's go for a walk."

Fine with me. Out of this place. Why don't you walk me to the train station? "Do you want to get a cup of coffee or something to eat?" I had a headache.

Stephan wanted only to walk. At arbitrary intervals he kicked stones along the pavement. *Say something, Stephan. I can't take the quiet anymore. I'm tired and I'm hungry.* "Are you sure you don't want some-

77

thing to eat?"

"No. I just want to walk. And think, you know."

Can't you think out loud a little? All this quiet is making me nervous. And I don't even want to be here. I don't want you to be sad. And I don't want to be dressed in black. I look lousy in black. "And I don't want your mother to be dead," I said.

"Oh Ruthie," Stephan said. "My poor Ruthie. Did you think I thought that?"

Stephan patted my head like I was a dog until I stopped blubbering. And then he pulled a fast one, asking me to have dinner with his family. Not on my toes, the only loophole I could grab on to was, "Are you sure it's all right?"

He said it was but it wasn't. His sisters were bustling around the kitchen trying to cook while Stephan and I got in the way. And then Stephan had to go to the bathroom. *You can't go and leave me alone out here. Can't I go with you? Can't you hold it in until after I've left?* But off he went leaving me shifting my weight back and forth in an attempt to look as if I were doing something other than standing there like a lump. One of the sisters thrust a batch of silverware in my hands.

"Oh? Set the table? I'd be glad to." I would have been delighted to set the table except that I promptly dropped the silverware on the floor. It was whisked up by another of the sisters who proceeded to wash it.

Stephan came out of the bathroom. "What was that crash?"

"Me. I dropped the silverware."

"Ruthie, do you want to go home?"

"Yes. I want to go home."

Stephan drove me to the train station. "I'm sorry I screwed up," I said. He told me I didn't screw up. I wanted to tell him he was a damned good sport to try and make me feel better when I was supposed to be making him feel better, but I didn't.

As the LIRR neared Penn Station, I finally found the words I'd been looking for and even though I was in a train and not a church or someplace like that, I figured I'd better tell Stephan's mother what was on my mind before I lost my thoughts again. And so I started to explain that I was sorry I didn't get to know her better and that she didn't get to know me because we might have gotten on just fine had we given the other a chance, when some runny-nosed kid in the seat behind me said, "Mommy, that lady's talking to herself."

"Shhh," the mother said, "the lady is praying."

Wheels

The door to my lab opens and Charlie pokes his head in. "You're not busy, are you?" he asks.

I give Charlie a look and tell him the truth. The only thing I've managed to do with any success this morning was button up my white coat. And even that took some trial and error. "My bacteria," I point to a pretty set of Fernbach flasks. "They died again, Charlie."

I'm supposed to be isolating enzymes from *E.coli* only my bacteria refuse to cooperate and insist on dying instead. The rest of my thesis is written in code on Tasty Kake wrappers. "I'm a mess," I say.

"Yes," Charlie concurs. "But never mind that

81

now. I've got something to show you."

I follow Charlie down the corridor and outside to the parking lot. He leads me past rows of Toyotas and Dodge Aspens and up to a cobalt blue Alfa Romeo. Circa 1980. The top is down and I swoon a little. "She's grand, Charlie. Whose is she?"

Charlie and I first met over an algae green '79 Jaguar XJ6 in this very parking lot. I was fawning over it, picturing myself in the driver's seat behind a pair of Foster Grants and breezing down a long stretch of highway with an unnatural blue sky overhead when Charlie happened by. He let go with what used to be called a wolf whistle and said, "What a beauty."

"Are you referring to me?" I asked. "Or do you mean the car?"

And Charlie said, "Oh, you're cute, too. Is the car yours?"

"In the fantasy I'm having, it is," I said.

Charlie came in close and ran his hands over the curves of the Jag's body. He leaned over and I thought for sure he was going to put his lips to the hood but he straightened up and asked, "Ever drive one of these?"

I shook my head and tried to figure out who this hot number was and why I'd never seen him around before. He wasn't in the Biology department, that was certain. The boys in the Bio. department were geeks.

"I drove one. Once," said Charlie. "It's like . . ." Words failed him so he let go with another whistle. A different kind of whistle. One that sounded like sailing and I thought to myself, "Here is a boy who knows cars."

We stood around cooing over the Jaguar for a time until I asked, "So, where do you come from?"

"Malta," he said. "I'm Maltese."

"Like the Maltese Falcon?" I asked.

And Charlie wanted to know, "Is that a car?"

Malta is a speck of an island bobbing in the Mediterranean like a cork. This is why Charlie's family hightailed it out of there. Charlie's father developed claustrophobia and Malta interfered with his breathing. Charlie said his father's lungs made noises like an engine with a broken fan belt. His father chose to come to America because in America, Charlie's father could drive for days and never see the edge. In America, Charlie's father did not hyperventilate.

The cobalt blue Alfa Romeo, Charlie tells me, is a rental. Neither Charlie nor I can keep a car in the city but we are on a first-name basis with quite a number of rent-a-car establishments around town. Charlie's wallet is thick with cards from Olins and Avis and Budget. I've dated boys who collected girls' phone numbers like that. "I got her from European International," Charlie says. "She's ours. For the day. So, climb in."

Charlie and I know perfectly well that I will give in but first I must play coy and resist. "I can't, Charlie," I say. "I want to. You know I want to but my lab is crawling with dead bacteria."

"Crawling with dead bacteria is oxymoronic." Charlie's got that infuriating precision of English common to a number of show-offs who've learned it as a second language. However, precision hasn't anything to do with passion and will not entice me into the cobalt blue Alfa Romeo. Driving is a near sexual experience and lusty. Charlie's voice gets husky as he coaxes. "Come on," he says. "How many chances will you get to ride around in a doll like this? I'll even let you take the wheel for a while. Maybe," he adds.

In a different set of circumstances this is the point where I'd be kicking off my shoes and unzipping my skirt. "Okay," I succumb. "But hang on a minute. I've got to lock up the lab. And go to the bathroom." Whenever Charlie and I go driving, I make it a point to use the bathroom beforehand. Twice, if I can, because pit stops, according to Charlie, make for an uneven ride and often he refuses.

I hurry back to the parking lot and Charlie, already planted in the driver's seat, gives the horn a couple of toots. The motor is purring. Instead of opening the door, I hop over it like you sometimes see in the movies. It's a neat little two-step.

Charlie burns rubber.

Driving in the city causes Charlie to grumble. Potholes, he says, are the blight of the age. He swears out loud as the Alfa Romeo whomps. "Potholes," Charlie waves his fist. "They're bruising her undercarriage."

Not that Charlie is always gentle with a car. I've seen him push a car to its limits and then some. Testing its endurance, forcing a clunker of a Chevy to extinction. Whispering, "Come on. Do it for me, baby," as he pushed the old geezer to reach eighty when it was clearly huffing at sixty. Or peeling out on a set of bald tires, asking them to be tough for him. Once, right after a giant of a snowstorm, Charlie and I got bit with the urge to drive so we rented a '73 Olds 98 with a 350 engine and snowtires. We were tooling around some place in the country, maybe upstate New York or Pennsylvania. This Olds was a trooper, never even coughed. Charlie was coursing the side roads when we came to one of those forks which are a staple of country driving. Charlie veered to the left.

Midway down the road, in deference to a twenty-three foot snow drift obstructing our path, Charlie put on his brakes. I rolled down the window and looked out. Other cars had made this same mistake. There were a number of tire tracks in the shape of a U-turn in the snow.

Charlie got out of the car and studied this phenomenon. He came back behind the wheel and said, "You know something? We should've been physicists. Physics," Charlie said, "has practical application." Licking his finger and using the windshield as a chalkboard, Charlie did a calculation. "Okay, that should do it," he said, and he put the Olds into reverse, backing it up maybe six yards. Then Charlie instructed, "Hold tight," and coming down full force on the gas, he floored the Olds and we plowed clear through the snow drift. The only other time I'd seen anything like it was in cartoons when Bugs Bunny made a quick getaway through a brick wall.

Outside the city we pick up Interstate 95. I think we're headed south but that's a detail we have no concern with. Direction is irrelevant to us. Charlie once confided to me that his fiance is very destination oriented. I never can remember the name of Charlie's fiance. She's a little thing. And blonde. Cute, if somewhat tight around the mouth. I call her Eunice, a random association. She hates that I call her Eunice no matter how many times I assure her there's nothing to it. "Everytime we get in a car," Charlie told me, "she wants to know where we are going. And then she asks how long until we're there. She needs to get some place," Charlie said.

And I said, "No kidding."

In his lab, over his array of flasks and beakers, Charlie has a pin-up of a Maserati. A red Maserati. "She's a bi-turbo," Charlie said practically lasciviously the first time he saw me looking at it. Charlie knows a lot more about the fine points of a car than I do. Charlie knows all about carburetors and PCV valves and spark plugs. He's been educating me about engines.

A few weeks ago, I popped in on Charlie to find him mooning over that pin-up of the Maserati the way teen-agers moon over *Playboy*'s Miss September.

Unable to take his eyes from the Maserati's headlights, Charlie asked me, "Do you ever wonder what you're doing here?"

Thinking of the failed experiment du jour I said, "Sure. All the time. It could be I'm not cut out to be a scientist. I'm not exact enough. I make mistakes. I lose things. But then I remember all the great discoveries made through error. Mold in petri dishes that weren't washed properly turning out to be antibodies to rare diseases, and I take heart. There's hope for me yet."

"And you imagine you'll save whole populations in Africa or India?" Charlie guessed.

I shrugged, embarrassed. "I'll probably end up teaching," I said. "Introduction to Biology and Anatomy. At some little college. I'll grow into a dirty old woman acquainting freshmen with the proper names for body parts," I snickered.

"You think you'll like that?" Charlie demanded of me although he didn't wait for an answer. Rather, it was as if he slipped out of the moment and was no longer talking to me when he continued. "I spend my days mixing gases with liquids and then standing around waiting to see how they react. They react but I just stand there and all the while I'm thinking about driving. Driving fast." Then he snapped back and asked me, "Did you ever go to the races?" Charlie told me when he was a boy his father took him to a Grand Prix. Charlie waxed on about getting behind the wheel of a car built close to the ground. About strapping yourself in to become a piece of equipment. About wearing a white jumpsuit and a crash helmet. About revving the engine of a Lamborghini until the flag is dropped. And then taking off like a bullet from a .38 and racing around and around the track. "The only destination," Charlie said, "is speed."

In less than two weeks Charlie is getting married to Eunice. On the following Monday, he is off to Industry. The grinds at American Cyanimid have scooped him up at a none too shabby salary. Instead of strapping himself in behind the wheel of a race car, Charlie will be strapping himself in behind a desk. He'll be wearing a tie and jacket, not a white jumpsuit, and because he won't be able to take a drive whenever he fancies, he'll grip his test tubes like a stick shift and make engine noises with his lips. His Bunsen burner will create minor explosions and Charlie will pretend they are the sound of backfire. Charlie has buckled up the safety belt in his life.

The Interstate is relatively free of traffic. Charlie shifts into third. We're coasting along at a steady seventy-five miles an hour, leaving the other cars on the road in the dust. A jaundiced yellow Karmann Ghia with rusted fenders tries to catch us. Our Alfa Romeo blows smoke in her face. "Aw Charlie," I say. "A Karmann Ghia." I get dewy. "I used to have a Karmann Ghia. My very first car."

"A Karmann Ghia," Charlie says, "handles like

a tank. You never get a smooth performance out of a Karmann Ghia."

"Oh Charlie," I'm sentimental, "I loved that car. She was white. With a black interior. And four on the floor. Her top rolled down with a hand crank and she had AM/FM stereo. My friends and I used to pile into her like clowns into a VW at the circus and drive the roads scouting for carloads of boys."

"A purist," Charlie condescends, "never has a motive for driving. The purist isn't scouting for anything."

"Be quiet and let me finish." I start to sound like I'm crying into a beer. "One dark night, Charlie, I was taking a sharp turn and I wrapped my Karmann Ghia around a tree. She was ruined. Demolished. Good only for the junkyard and I walked away without a scratch on me. The injustice of it all. The anguish."

"Yeah, well," Charlie concedes, "your first car is always special, I guess."

When it comes to state police, Charlie has got a sixth sense. His antennae pick up the law and he eases the Alfa Romeo into a fifty-five crawl. We poke along, Charlie keeping one eye on the rearview mirror. He is antsy and raring to go. He jiggles in his seat.

When we're out of the radar zone, Charlie gives an all-clear signal and puts pressure on the gas pedal. The pick-up on this car is split-second. Charlie claims she can do 0 to 110 in three. I don't doubt it.

I lean back against the cream-colored seat and

ask Charlie, "Do you know Stan Ackerman? He's in the lab down the hall from me? He's doing Post Doc? You must've seen him around. He's the guy with eyes the exact color as this cobalt blue Alfa Romeo."

Charlie doesn't know who I mean.

"You must know who he is," I say. "His eyes make my knees wobble."

"That means nothing to me," Charlie sounds snitty, maybe because that's how I get when he talks about Eunice.

I tell Charlie how I had more than a professional interest in Ackerman. "I was crazy for the guy but then I found out he's doing work on cloning. Do you think cloning is immoral?" I ask.

"Morality is not the scientist's concern," Charlie parrots an old argument about how we're not responsible for what society does with our formulae. It's not an argument I'm completely comfortable with.

"The other day," I say, "I went to Ackerman's office intending to throw myself at him and he put his arm around me and pulled me close like he was going to kiss me, but instead he whispered in my ear that he could make twin frogs. One on one day and the other one next week or next year or whenever he chooses. Don't you think that's kind of creepy? I'm not sure I want to make it with some guy who's creating twin frogs."

"Oh, I don't know," Charlie says. "Think about it. If you were cloned you could be here with me now in this car and at the same time be back in your lab sentencing more bacteria to their deaths."

"And you, " I say, "could walk down the aisle while driving on the Santa Monica Freeway." Driving the Santa Monica Freeway has always been one of Charlie's goals. I expect him to take to this picture but he doesn't say anything.

Charlie fiddles with the radio and then snaps it off. I fish around in the bottom of my pocketbook and bring up two pieces of bubble gum. I pick off some lint that has stuck to the wrappers and ask Charlie if he wants a piece. I unwrap it for him and put it in his mouth. We both chew hard. The gum is old but it's sweet and pink and chewing it clears my mind of all things other than bubble gum and cruising in a convertible. Charlie chomps on his once more and says, "This stuff's like an old tire." He takes it out with a thumb and index finger and holds it out for me. "Get rid of this, will you?" he asks.

I take the wad of gum from him and let the wind pick it up.

An exit sign, Exit 76 Oakdale, catches my attention and I ask, "Are we by any chance in New Jersey?"

"I think so," Charlie says. "We're on the Jersey Turnpike."

"I know a girl who lives here. Here, in Oakdale."

"You don't want to stop, do you?" Charlie is appalled at the very idea.

"No," I say. "This girl, she moved to Oakdale because she fell in love with a convict she met through a personal ad. He was in prison around here. She wanted to be closer to the jail."

"Jail," Charlie shudders as if he's been there and he gives the car more juice.

Once, Charlie and I went shopping at the Ferrari showroom. We were a convincing enough pair that the salesman let us take one, a silver one, for a test drive. Charlie test drove that Ferrari for twenty-six miles going and twenty-eight miles back. When we finally pulled into the showroom, the salesman was in a pet. Pacing the carpeted floor and mopping sweat off his neck, he threatened to call the police and have us arrested. Later, Charlie said that was one of the finest drives of his life. "The only thing that could be better," Charlie said, "would be a spin in a Lamborghini." Charlie pronounces "Lamborghini" like an Italian.

Charlie's got the Alfa Romeo doing ninety. Whizzing along the highway, the scenery blurs. The trees won't hold form. My hair whips against my face. What a swell car this is. She's not even sweating. "You know, Charlie," I say, "we ought to get one of these. We ought to get ourselves a cobalt blue Alfa Romeo. We could afford it maybe if we went partners. We could keep her in the university lot and I know we wouldn't squabble over her because we always go driving together anyway. What do you think?"

"I think it's a nice idea," Charlie says.

And then I remember American Cyanimid is located in Connecticut and Charlie and Eunice have recently acquired a mortgage on a house out there.

"Nice ideas," Charlie repeats with a sigh. "So many nice ideas."

Another nice idea would be to tell Charlie he doesn't have to go through with his plans. People can change their minds. Just because the wheels are in motion is no reason not to switch gears or take a turn. He ought to go in halves on a car with me. Then, we could drive and drive, drive off into the sunset and over the horizon but I don't say any of that. Instead I tell Charlie about a man in Texas who is dead and buried upright behind the wheel of his Lincoln Continental.

"Yeah," says Charlie, "I can appreciate that. The Lincoln is a good car."

I aim to ease away some of Charlie's sadness and point out that Connecticut is a place tailor-made for driving. "The whole state is packed with thruways and highways and back roads and side streets and three car families. You can keep a car there with no problem. So, what kind of car are you going to get?"

Charlie mumbles something. I ask him to repeat that and he says, "I've already got one."

I get to thinking this cobalt blue Alfa Romeo isn't a rental after all. Charlie's been holding out on me. "It is, isn't it?" I ask. "This is your car?"

"No," says Charlie and he adds, "I wish." He confesses that Eunice has bought him a car. As a wedding gift. One she picked out herself. "A Honda Civic," he says.

"A Honda Civic? You call that a car?"

"No," says Charlie. "I don't call that a car. I hate those Japanese buggies. They're made out of tin. They behave like Tonka Toys."

I feel lousy for Charlie being saddled with a Honda Civic. I try to make it sound a little attractive and mention they are good on gas.

But Charlie doesn't want me to make it sound attractive. "It's grey," he tells me, knowing I'll loathe the color. Somebody ought to straighten Eunice out about cars. But that is Charlie's onus.

As the subject of gas has come up, I peer over at the gauge and note it is hovering just over E. "We need petrol," I say. "Petrol" is a term I picked up from Charlie only he uses it synonymously with gasoline whereas I use it to connote prestige. The way I use it, it's okay to put gas in a Ford Granada or a Dodge Charger or a Volkswagen Rabbit, but an Alfa Romeo deserves petrol, if not perfume, in her tank.

Charlie resents having to stop for fuel. He often talks about designing a tank which could be filled merely by pressing a button on the dash board. "How is it you always remember to feed a car but forget to feed your bacteria?" Charlie makes it sound like it's my fault we have to stop.

I don't forget to feed my bacteria. What I forget is to add the magnesium to the gruel. I forget bacteria need magnesium because, to me, magnesium is a forgettable element. "It's a matter of priorities," I tell Charlie.

There is a Mobil station ahead and Charlie drives in. He pulls the Alfa Romeo up to the pump. Charlie is impatient and honks the horn for service. The gas station attendant comes up to the car. He is wearing a pair of those white coveralls which Charlie covets. His name is embroidered in red over the right pocket. "Ed," it says.

Ed is a knockout. And suntanned. By comparison, Charlie and I look awfully pale, like a couple of stiffs. Ed is causing my heartbeat to accelerate, my pulse to race.

Ed's fingers touch the Alfa Romeo's door, lightly. He says to Charlie, "Fantastic automobile you've got there."

I elbow Charlie in the ribs. "Charlie, he's got the same eyes as Ackerman. I'm turning to mush."

Charlie pays me no attention and tells Ed to fill her up. "Super unleaded, right?" Ed asks. And Charlie says, "Of course."

"Just checking. You would not believe," Ed tells us, "what some people put in their cars just to save a few pennies." He rolls his eyeballs. I follow his irises hoping to make contact.

While the Alfa Romeo is refueling, Ed hovers around. "Really a beauty," he says.

"Charlie," I whisper. "Ackerman's eyes on a car

95

freak. I want this boy, Charlie."

"Aficionado," Charlie tells me. "Not car freak. Aficionado."

"Whatever. Don't bog me down with semantics. Help me out here."

Charlie is a good sport. "Ever drive one of these?" he asks Ed.

"Yeah. A couple of times." Ed tells us he works weekends as a mechanic at Devon. The race track. "So I get to give the cars a test run. Once," he mentions, "I got to test drive a Lamborghini. Nothing like that in the world."

It is Charlie's turn to be wowed.

When the tank is full Ed takes our money and goes off to the garage to make change. Charlie turns to me and says, "He drove a Lamborghini. I never met anyone who drove a Lamborghini before."

"Love at the pumps," I say.

Ed comes back and counts out four singles. "Really a great car," he says again. "And you've got yourselves the perfect day for a drive."

"Hey," Charlie asks, "you want to come along?" This is an unprecedented burst of brilliance on Charlie's part. I give Charlie a thumbs up and say, "Yeah, Ed. Come along. Please. Do. Please do. Yeah. Come along," until Charlie tells me to quit acting like a dog panting out the rear window.

We chalk up another point in Ed's favor as he does not ask where we're headed. Instead, he looks over at the garage and back to the Alfa Romeo and says, "Sure. Why not?" He hops in the car the way I did. Like a pro, only he sits on the edge of the trunk. His legs fit in that space meant for luggage.

I twist around to face Ed. He winks at me. I blow a pink bubble for him and I think we're like three outlaws in our getaway car. I think we ought to be wearing hats.

"Tell me," Charlie asks Ed, "how fast could that Lamborghini go?" And Ed tells us, "As quick as a dream."

Charlie takes that in. He turns the ignition key and puts our cobalt blue Alfa Romeo into high gear. "Hold tight," Charlie says.

Red Fever

It is probably not a good idea to write about lovesickness while ailing; not much chance for that clearheaded, detached, objectivity that's in vogue. But I don't have much of a choice. It's either this or I listen to *Leslie Gore's Greatest Hits* for the twenty-second time in succession. And even I, who might very well be Leslie's greatest, all time, long standing fan, might not be able to stomach another encore of "Sunshine, Lollipops and Rainbows." Do not, for a moment, think I've squandered these hours with my ear cocked to the stereo. I did make a discovery. Due to my own malaise, it occurred to me that Judy, of "It's Judy's Turn to Cry" fame, was not the cunt she was made out to be. She was willing to, and did, ruin her reputation (her most precious commodity) only because of her love for Johnny. Everyone hated her for her inability to yield but that didn't stop her. Judy was my kind of woman.

I know. I'm off the track, not sticking to the point, babbling, rambling, beating around the proverbial beaten around bush. But it's easier to write about Judy and Johnny because, hell, I don't even know Judy and Johnny. Quite frankly, I'm not sure I'm keen on committing to paper the fact that I've been spending my days slithering around on the floor.

I am not an adolescent, yet how do I explain the piece of paper with our names, mine and his, written inside a lopsided heart; the obligatory arrow piercing us together? And beneath that I have written our names again. Playing that teenage game of crossing out the common letters and with what remains, chanting, "Love. Hate. Love. Hate. Love. Hate." I don't. I tear the paper into strips and eat them.

This stimulates my appetite for the first time in days. I open a can of Campbell's Chicken and Rice. Grabbing a spoon but neglecting a bowl, I eat the goop, lukewarm, from the pot. Halfway through, I change my mind and dump the rest into the toilet. Although I know the sight of dirty dishes does nothing to ease despair, washing the pot and spoon proves too much for me. I solve the dilemma by hiding them in the refrigerator.

Yesterday, I had to go out. I did not want to, preferring the confines of my apartment. Privacy is more suitable for moaning and pissing about.

It wasn't as bad out there as I had thought it would be until I followed a man because of the cigarette he smoked. Not stopping to think about why, I followed him for four blocks, sniffing after him and his aroma. Like Pavlov's dog cued by the smoke, my tail went up and I grew moist between the thighs. I might have jumped on him but then he flicked the remains of his cigarette into a puddle and lost his allure.

I scurried off and bought a pack of that very same brand. As I sit here now, I've got one going in the ashtray. I don't smoke them. I just keep lighting them to smell them as they burn.

Because he hasn't called me, I suspect my phone is out of order. I suspect the telephone company, in connection with the government, of masterminding a plot to keep the cogs turning by shutting off our phones at crucial times. They've got us wired up to a giant electrocardiogram and when our hearts begin to pitter patter, Bingo! our phones go dead. I call the operator. "All right," I tell her. "I know what you people are up to. I'm supposed to forget all this and go back to work, right? Nice try but sorry. Enough is enough. I've suffered. So, could you please turn my phone back on now?"

She'll check it for me. So she says. I don't count on this as orders are orders and I don't care what anyone says about Germans, Americans are the all-time order takers. Oh, she'll pretend to check on it. No need to ruffle the citizens.

Americans don't really have much use for love. Oh, we say we do when speaking in generalities. But deep inside we think it's subversive, gums up the works. We don't admit this and we continue to write books about passion, sing songs about romance, and once in a while we endow a university with a sizable grant to study love. But we don't revel in it. Our national sport is jogging and no American man ever chucked the chance to be king on account of a girl. We like our love in moderation. The wallowing sort is just not apple pie. We sneer at it as a weakness. We could not possibly worship love and then invent, succumb to, pantyhose. Control Top Pantyhose; why, the very name prohibits abandon.

For me to admit my lovesickness, well, I might as well say I've got Red Fever, Pinko Pox. Our heritage is independence and we are a generation of patriotic, stalwart stoics. We keep stiff upper lips instead of soft, moist ones. Even the women, now, take pride in their inability to surrender.

I could run off and join the Foreign Legion.

My phone rings and I trip over myself to get to it. The operator informs me my phone is in working order. "Yeah. Order, all right," I say.

"Excuse me, ma'am?"

"Nothing. I know. You're doing your job."

I'm not blind to the fact that I am a trifle guilty of the same brand of cowardice my peers are guilty of

— fear of being scoffed at. I may not be afraid to get lovesickness or admit to having it, when asked, but I have not run through the streets announcing it, proclaiming my dependence. I should be dragging myself along the concrete letting the crowds witness my consumption, proudly raising my shackled wrists. But that sort of thing just isn't done anymore. Pity, I'll grant, but I'm not up to revolutionizing our outlook. I have a hard enough time lifting myself out of bed.

I could get a cat. A nice, aristocratic Persian whose white hairs would cling to my mourning clothes, further demonstrating how far gone I am, not caring enough to brush myself off. The white pussy would sit on my lap asking only for a scratch behind the ears or under the chin, in return for which she would listen to me as I wail. I could tell her everything about him, every saccharine detail and she would purr and ching. Her unblinking eyes staring up in disgust, perhaps, at my outpouring of slop but I could pretend she is sympathetic. A pussy could be a comfort in times like this. I think about this some more but then remember if I do not perish from this illness, I'd be stuck cleaning out a litter box thrice weekly, a task I do not think I am well suited for.

Maybe I'll take up the harp, stand outside his window and pick an ethereal tune or two.

A futile five minutes is spent trying to talk myself out of loving him. I list all his faults, all his downfallings:

1. mousey-colored hair
2. pretentions
   a) imported cigarettes
   b) French wines only. Turned up
   his far from perfect nose at the
   Italian burgundy I bought
   c) goes to "the films" a lot
3. sweaty palms
4. kisses with "too much teeth"
5. scrawny chest
6. nearsighted
7. myopic
8. does not have the good sense
   to love me back
9. says he is "too busy"

That last one slays me. Another slice of American propaganda: keep "too busy." Desire is counterproductive. There is no love in the afternoon for us. No siestas. We have to wait until night when we are too tired. If we made love all afternoon, who would man the assembly lines?

But I know trying to talk myself out of loving someone is as useless as talking myself into loving someone.

I list the reasons I do love him but I wouldn't think of reproducing them here. I am not about to force-feed slosh down anyone's throat.

I wonder if he knows he is feeding off my vital

organs and ruining my health.

Curled up on the couch, I think about eating chocolates. Truffles would be nice; Elysian chocolates to titillate the senses. But I don't want to go out for them. I'll have to make do dreaming about them.

My phone rings again and I springboard across the room. "Hello?"

It is Newt. Newt is a poet who whines a lot. I'm not up for talking to Newt now as I'm whining enough for a whole platoon of afflicted persons. Newt writes technically perfect poems, rhythmic and metric exactitudes that don't say much. "I never write from any kind of personal experience," Newt has been known to brag.

"What do you want?" I ask. "You've got sixty seconds."

"This might take longer." I can hear his shoulders sag. "Why? Are you busy?"

"In a fashion. I'm sick, Newt."

"Oh. I want to ask you about love. How do you know the difference between real love and say, a crush or infatuation?"

Newt has got a decade of life on me and still he asks questions like that. "There's no difference, Newt. Crushes and infatuation are terms applied to teenagers to prevent them from running off and getting married at fourteen."

"Then how do you know what love is?"

"Excuse me?" He did not have to repeat himself. I did hear right. "Newt, you are thirty-five years old.

Haven't you ever been in love?"

"I don't know. What does it feel like? I mean, I might have been but I didn't know it. I guess I'm supposed to feel tragic now. But I don't feel tragic."

"Newt," I ask, "did you ever step in dog shit?" I have the feeling Newt steps in dog shit all the time.

"What's that got to do with anything?"

"You scrape and scrape at the bottom of your shoe but you never quite get it off? That's love, Newt."

Newt does not think that is a good poetic image. He wants this information to write a poem. Can't I come up with something better, he wants to know.

I could have invited him over to watch me in action as I pummel the walls with my fists and bray like a donkey, but I don't think he'd find that poetic, either. Maybe I'll invite him over tomorrow. By tomorrow, I should be pale and wan and somewhat thinner. I can stretch out on the couch for him, a cold compress on my forehead, and dab at my eyes with a silk hankie. If Newt will agree to bring me chocolate truffles and a fresh pack of Players, I might let him come by and observe that phase of the illness.

If we were really a civilized society, we would dispense with elementary school primers and make Proust the mandatory reading. Anna Karenina and Young Werther should replace Dick and Jane, Emma Bovary and Aschenbach filling the slots vacated by Spot and Puff. Catch the tykes early before the weariness sets in, before they catch a whiff of the stigma attached. When this illness strikes, they should know what it is and why it should be given in to. There should be some sort of rebellion against this prejudice against lovesickness.

A feel-good therapy-oriented acquaintance of mine, having just read an article entitled "Alone and Loving It," advised me, "Forget him. You've got to be strong and just walk away." But that's backwards. It doesn't take any strength to walk away. It's sticking with it, refusing the cures, refusing to keep busy and join clubs, that's the hard part. Like a gangrene victim, I welcome the ache. As long as it hurts, I know it's still there.

With all the smugness of John Wayne, as he turns down the shot of whiskey while the doc probes for the bullet, I flick on my stereo. Leslie sings. I clutch the pang with my left hand and dance around my apartment.

Money Honey

What they are trying to do is swindle Uncle Max. My father, his sisters and his brother and cousins have congregated in my parents' livingroom to eat cheese Danish by the pound, drink coffee laced with cream and Nutra Sweet, and devise a legal scheme to take for themselves Uncle Max's share of the inheritance. I happen to be here because I've left my husband and haven't, for the moment, any place to go. My Uncle Marty's boy Alex, a third-year law student at Cardoza, is giving free advice. I take a swallow of wine and try to picture Alex with a woman.

The situation is: My Great Uncle Jack died and left a mattress full of money to no one in particular. This money comes to the tune of 2.97 million dollars, not an amount you'd sneeze at. Everyone knew Jack had some money socked away because he made a decent living and never spent five cents. But no one knew it was that much money; not even my Aunt Pauline who has always concerned herself with Jack's bank accounts.

Pauline believed she was most deserving of whatever money Jack had to leave behind because she had the most miserable life in the family. A little money might ease her sorrows. Pauline's miserable life is an often discussed epic at family get-togethers. Most often, it is Pauline who brings the subject up. She thrives on retelling the story of how her husband was a gambler who took up with a taxi dancer, leaving Pauline and the twins without a dollar. Pauline slaved as a bookkeeper to feed and clothe the twins who turned out to be a pair of ingrates. Having inherited their father's ways, they flew the coop as soon as they were able to and never call Pauline to say so much as hello.

As if that were not enough misery for any one person, Pauline finally met a very nice man to keep company with. For seven years she cooked him dinner and pressed his shorts, when he upped and decided he didn't care much for Pauline. From Aunt Pauline I have learned that men aren't too interested in having their underwear ironed.

Getting dumped is a family trait. I come from a family of rejects who are always getting ditched when love comes calling. I'm the first one, that anyone can remember, who did the jilting. When I walked out on Bernie, which was only seven weeks ago, Aunt Esther came over and pronounced that I had Ruth's genes.

"That's not possible, Aunt Esther," I said. "Ruth wasn't a blood relative."

Ruth was Louie's wife. She ran off with the butcher in 1954. She was forty-five. I'm the only one in the family who doesn't make a spitting gesture when her name is mentioned. Even though I never met her, she is my favorite aunt. The rest of the family calls her names, the same names they're calling me now, and ask, "How could she have left two little boys like that?" No one recognizes that her two little boys, Cecil and Stanley, were grown men with wives of their own when Ruth fell in love and decided to do something about it. Cecil's wife, in 1967, joined a commune in Vermont and divorced him by walking around a chicken three times under a full moon.

"No one in our family," Esther said to me, "walks out on a marriage."

The lawyer handling Uncle Jack's estate, not my cousin Alex, had explained the procedure for distributing the goods when no will has been drawn up. For several weeks, Pauline refused to accept the fact that there was no will. She had the lawyer comb Uncle Jack's apartment, slashing canvas and tapping at walls, certain that Jack bequeathed the money to her, some-where, somehow. "I was the only one who cared about him," she said. Pauline used to call Uncle Jack once a week to see if he were dead yet. "To check on his health," was the way she put it. When no will was uncovered, Pauline took to calling the lawyer "that shyster." As Uncle Jack never married, his money, after the government and the shyster take their pieces of the pie, is to be divided equally among his three brothers.

Of Jack's three brothers, two are dead. One of the dead ones would have been my grandfather if he didn't get knocked down and killed by a milk truck the year before I was born. The other dead brother was Louis, the one Ruth ran out on. He drowned in the surf at Coney Island in 1969. The lawyer had explained that Louie's sons Cecil and Stanley get to share his portion of the inheritance just as my father, Pauline, Esther and Marty will split their father's portion. At this moment, my father, Pauline, Esther and Marty are wishing heart attacks on each other.

The big winner in this jackpot is Uncle Max, Jack's living brother. He gets his third all to himself. Max married for the first time some ten years ago when he was seventy. He married Shirley, a widow with three grown children, he met at the counter of a luncheonette.

"I was Jack's favorite," Pauline says lighting up her third Winston 100 in half an hour. Pauline is a chainsmoker who has polyps on her throat and a whopping smoker's cough.

No one is paying any attention to Pauline's whining because the bone of contention today is Max who, as they see it, does not deserve such a sizable share of this money. He didn't like Jack any better than any of them did.

"I called Jack once a week," Pauline says. "Toll calls, too. That ought to be worth something."

"Aunt Pauline," Marty's boy Alex says, "you can't get reimbursed for the phone calls now."

"Which," Marty pipes in, "you only made in the first place trying to get into Jack's good graces. Hah."

Stanley brings the talk back to the agenda intended. "Max is an old man," he says. "He doesn't need that money for anything. I've got kids in college. Private college. Do you know what that costs today?"

"The point is," my father says, "now that Max has got a wife, who is a much younger woman, should he pass on, the money would go to her and her children by a previous marriage to a stranger. The money should not leave the family," my father says, as if this cash has great sentimental value.

For our second wedding anniversary, Bernie gave me a thousand dollars. Ten spanking new one hundred dollar bills in an envelope. He kissed me on the cheek and said, "This is for you to do whatever you wish. Happy anniversary." I put the thousand dollars in the food processor, which I diced up along with some onions and green peppers. I made a meatloaf and didn't tell Bernie that he'd eaten his money until after he'd climbed off of me in bed two nights later.

I get up to get more wine. My mother is in the

kitchen putting up a fresh pot of coffee. "You should go easy on that, maybe," she says as I refill my glass.

"And listen to that stone cold sober?" I cock my thumb towards the livingroom. "Are you crazy?"

I settle back into the sofa as my father is saying, "We'll explain it to him. He'll understand. What would he do with so much money anyway?"

"Sure," Esther says, "Max will turn over a million dollars just like that."

Earlier on, Esther showed me a list she'd written out of what she was going to do with her pile of money. Esther wants a sable coat and a trip to Hawaii. Also, she wants box seats for the opera. I told Aunt Esther her list was very nice, which must have given her the impression she could talk to me. Esther sat down next to me and put her arm around my waist in a motherly fashion and said, "When are you going to quit acting like a silly little girl? Do you know what you're doing to your parents? Go back to Bernie. Make everyone happy."

"But I don't love Bernie, Aunt Esther," I said, easing myself out of her clutches.

"So? What's that got to do with anything? Love. You'll learn to love him. Look where love got Pauline." Esther made a face like she smelled something sour. "Who needs love? Bernie gave you a good life. Be grateful."

The night I had done with Bernie, Aunt Esther, who can smell trouble from two blocks away, came rushing over, her hair in rollers, to join in on the powwow. All I wanted to do was go to sleep, having left Bernie just before midnight, but the three of them, my parents and Esther, fed me coffee and question after question. "Does he beat you? Does he drink? Does he gamble? Does he provide for you? He takes you out to dinner?"

"He's lousy in bed," I said. My father got up and left the room. "And he's getting fat. He's only twenty-eight years old and already he's plump. I'm not attracted to plump men."

"There is more than that to a marriage." My mother couldn't bring herself to say "sex."

"She's got Ruth's genes," Aunt Esther was certain.

"So he's a little chubby," my mother said. "More of him to love."

And I said, "But I don't love him at all."

Marty's boy Alex is showing himself to be a first-rate slime. He's come up with the idea of having Uncle Max declared insane. "You know," he says, "we produce evidence of some crazy stuff he's done and bring it before a judge. We get him committed and one of us becomes executor of his estate and handles his money accordingly."

"Us?" I ask Alex. "What's with this 'us' business? None of this money is yours until Marty here croaks."

A line of sweat breaks out on Alex's upper lip.

115

"I mean," he says, "the people I am representing."

"Representing, are we?" Alex is such an easy victim, it's almost no fun. "Isn't there some funny little rule against practicing law without a license? Perhaps I ought to give the Bar a call."

"Don't pay any attention to her," my father says. "A woman who leaves her husband . . ." The rest of his thoughts get stuck in his throat.

"Besides," Marty says, "she's been drinking."

I make a toast in Marty's direction and empty my wine glass in a defiant gulp.

My mother is sitting at the kitchen table looking worried. I have a hunch she isn't liking this either, only she would never say so. "Do you hear what's going on out there?" I ask. "They're vultures."

"Shh," my mother says. "Your own family. You shouldn't talk like that."

My own family, only I'm closer in kind to the wayward in-laws, the ones I never met or don't remember. My own family treats me now like I'm from the other side. Which I guess I am. I don't feel related to these people who equate love with obligation, who tell me I have to settle. It is no mystery to me why Ruth and Pauline's men lit out. "I shouldn't talk like that?" I say to my mother. "They're out there talking about having Max committed to an insane asylum so they can get their grubby mitts on a few lousy dollars."

My mother clamps her hands over her ears. I

open a fresh bottle of wine and if my mother had another set of hands, surely she would use them to cover her eyes. Last night my mother came into my room and said, "Maybe love isn't what you thought it would be. Maybe it's not Bernie who isn't so hot. What do you know from how it's supposed to be?"

I knew my mother wasn't ready to hear my answer but I've learned that no one is ever ready to hear what they call bad news. There is no good time to tell your mother you've had a string of lovers and there is no good time to dump your husband. "I don't want to hear any more," my mother had said.

I think about being the one to come to Uncle Max's rescue; standing guard over him, not letting any of them near him. Telling them they'd have to get to me first. I picture the courtroom, all the relatives on one side, pop-eyed with greed; Max and I the underdogs fighting for justice. I'd prove to the jury that Uncle Max is as sane as they are and that his nieces and nephews are but a pack of hyenas feeding off the dead and the elderly. I think I saw this in a movie because the truth is that sort of selflessness wouldn't come to me on my own. I don't know as I care for Uncle Max any more than I care for any of my relatives. I hardly know Uncle Max. All I remember about him is his large ears which don't do him an ounce of good. When Marty called Uncle Max to tell him about Jack's death, Max said, "What?" Max is deaf enough to not hear himself pass gas. He doesn't hear it so he assumes no one else does either. Uncle Max is not the cuddly kind of old person. I wouldn't want to spend any time with him no matter what.

The real reason I'm so up in arms over what they're plotting out there is it gives me an excuse to find fault with them. To even up the score.

They tell me I've broken Bernie's heart; that I've done the unforgivable. I've walked out on a perfectly good marriage. Never mind that if it really was perfectly good I would not have taken a powder. They tell me I've trampled all over Bernie's dreams. I've ruined him. My parents adore Bernie. My father says Bernie is the son he didn't have, his heir. My mother calls Bernie a prince, a king. He's everything they could have wanted for me. So sweet, is Bernie.

Bernie is such a marshmallow that I couldn't get him to throw me out no matter how I provoked him. I had to leave him because he wouldn't leave me. During the two and a half years I was married to Bernie, I had four affairs which I happened to mention when I told Bernie I wanted out. I had one affair with an old boyfriend of mine, another one with a man I met at a party who slipped me his phone number along with a fried zucchini stick. Then there was that fling with the man who fixed my car at the garage. The fourth affair was with Bernie's friend Jonathan. That was the one I told him about when he asked, "Who with?"

Well, at least I wouldn't try to swindle an old man out of a little bit of money.

"Why did you marry me in the first place?" Bernie asked and I said, "Bernie, that is a question I ask myself every single day."

They are all liking the scheme of having Max declared incompetent. What they are trying to do now is come up with stories about Max, stories which will establish him as crazy. Except this is not so easy, as Max isn't even eccentric. Their stories are feeble and prove nothing but their desperation. They have, actually, missed their best shot at going for this treasure. Pity they didn't think of this scheme a year ago when Jack was alive. With Jack, they might have had a case. A millionaire three times over who lived in a nearly condemned ramshackle building, a recluse who probably ate dog food, they could have channeled Jack through the courts and into Bellevue. Too late now, folks. I find myself wishing Jack had willed his money to a pet canary.

With one still burning in the ashtray, Pauline lights another cigarette. "There was that time he wandered out of Elaine's wedding and hooked up with a stranger's testimonial dinner in the next hall," she says.

"I don't know whether to pity you," I say, "or despise you."

"Oh," my father says, "and I suppose if someone were going to give you money, you would refuse it."

"I fail to make the connection," I say. "No one is giving you anything. You're stealing."

"You send her off to that fancy college," Pauline says, "look how she turns out."

There is a physical resemblance between Pauline and me. I have her eyes and pouting mouth. I look like I could be Pauline's daughter. It's always said that Pauline was the beauty in the family until bitterness and cigarettes and overeating won out. I wonder how many affairs her husband had before he made off with the taxi dancer.

I'm tipsy enough to think about seducing Marty's boy Alex. Purely out of spite.

Bernie was a virgin the first time we made love. I don't think I ever forgave him for that. I thought it such a defect, and I pitied him for it, the sort of pity which mushrooms into disgust.

My mother comes out of the kitchen carrying a tray of turkey sandwiches. "It's almost dinner time," she says. "You all must be hungry." She sets the tray down on the coffee table.

"They don't want your turkey sandwiches," I say to my mother. "This crowd is after blood. Why don't you slit open your veins for them? That ought to make them happy."

No one thanks my mother for the food but they do make a bee-line for it, grabbing sandwiches and talking with their mouths full, claiming they are too upset to eat.

My mother joins me on the sofa and says to me, "I know it looks like they're not being very nice. But try to see it from their side. No one has had an easy life. It's not right that you sit here criticizing."

"Getting more money isn't going to make them happy," I say.

"And what about you?" my mother asks. "What will it take to make you happy?"

"I don't know," I tell her.

Stanley's wife is wrapping up a turkey sandwich to take home. I want to laugh but I can't find it.

Marty asks if anyone has talked to Max about a will. Marty's latest idea is that they should guide Uncle Max's hand in such a way as to cut his wife out of any money left by Jack. "Max might go for that," he says. "And provided he doesn't go on some wild spending spree, it'll just be sitting there collecting interest and waiting for us."

I told Bernie I was leaving him during sex.

The telephone rings and my mother goes back to the kitchen to answer it. For the first few weeks, Bernie was calling here every day. I wouldn't speak to him, so instead he talked to my mother and my father, asking them to relay messages, messages asking me to be sensible and come back. Bernie whined to my family, which I didn't think at all fair.

My mother signals me into the kitchen. She is holding the receiver out to me and says, "It's Bernie. Go on, talk to him. It couldn't hurt just to talk."

I take the phone and say hello into it.

"I'm filing for divorce," Bernie says.

121

I tell him that is a good plan. "It wasn't going to work out, Bernie," I say.

"I'm filing for divorce on the grounds of adultery," Bernie says. "On my attorney's advice."

"Yeah, well. That's fair."

Bernie cracks up over the phone. His voice breaks. "You're not getting anything from me. Do you understand that? I'm not giving you alimony. Nothing. You can't have anything. No settlement. You'll pay for this. Nothing. Not the house or the furniture. I'm keeping all of it. I'm keeping the wedding presents too. I won't give you a penny. Do you understand? I want you to suffer." Bernie does not wait for me to respond. He hangs up on me.

I keep the phone next to my ear and listen to the dial tone. From the livingroom I hear my Aunt Pauline say, "I don't have anything. I should at least have some money."

A Feast of Reality

Julian telephones me from his office. Julian teaches English Composition at the Fashion Institute of Technology. His students are not very bright but often they are quite the little knockouts. If I were a man, I would want to teach English Composition at the Fashion Institute of Technology. Julian hates his job. "Oh good. You're home," he says and invites me out to dinner.

I don't want to have dinner with Julian. He's a drain, always depressed over nothing we can pin down. I tell him I can't go out to eat. "I'm broke, Julian. Sorry."

"But I have to talk to you," and he offers to spring for dinner. I'm a regular whore when it comes to a free meal and so I say okay.

Julian is usually depressed over what he calls his alienation. Who told him to move to Brooklyn, is the way I see it. No one wants to ride the F train at night. Julian claims there is more to it than that but when I ask what, there is never an answer. "Everything," he says.

Tonight, sitting across the table from me, Julian has fingered the problem. He is lonely. He has a solution. He wants to be in love. With me. "I want a relationship," Julian says.

I would no more want a relationship than I would want to fall in love with a person who chooses that word. "A relationship?" I say. "Isn't that what the United States has with Red China?"

"Come on. I'm serious." How redundant. Julian is always serious. "I want a relationship."

"With someone," I say.

"Of course with someone." Julian is looking at me as if I've come unhinged. "I'm tired of being alone." He thinks he's clarifying, when he has, in fact, missed my point.

"Someone. Anyone. Any girl would do."

"Not just anyone." Julian does have standards. Any girl with the particular properties he considers necessary, is what he means. It doesn't have to be me. Julian reacts to my expression and says, "I want it to be you." He thinks this is beguiling.

Conscious of being in a public place or too lily-livered to make any kind of a move without my first granting permission, Julian employs both hands to eat his hamburger instead of leaving one free to grope under the table for my thigh. This is another reason I would never love Julian.

"And what do you expect from this," I swallow a piece of veal along with the word, "relationship?"

Julian is not about to compromise himself. He shrugs his shoulders and says, "You know."

"No, Julian. I don't know. I've never had a relationship. I fall in love."

He tells me that is the same thing.

Some weeks ago, in one of those coffee houses Julian is so partial to, we sat drinking tea (of all things) and discussed the three phases of love. The first phase, we'd decided, was all romantic fire, passion, indulgence. When it is easier to be together than not is phase two. The third phase, which Julian thought the best, and I coined "the wheelchair phase," is when life together is a series of memories and love takes on the comforting glow of a night light.

We'd argued for several futile hours as I tried to explain to him that it was the first phase, and that first phase only, which captures my attention. When I catch a whiff of the stench of phase two, I take off.

"That's twisted," Julian said.

"Maybe. But that's the way I like it."

"You leave them," he snapped his fingers, "just like that? Good-bye, sucker. I never want to see you again." Julian was horrified. He said I had no sense of obligation but to me, once obligation enters the picture, the love is done for, anyway. Why stick around for chemotherapy?

"But that's not reality," Julian said.

I reminded Julian of a professor we had in college who convinced us the chairs we were sitting on did not exist.

"College isn't reality, either," Julian had said.

I loathe having my reality defined for me. So I walked off on him.

Julian wants to measure time in pencil markings on the kitchen wall and when the kiddies reach five feet, Julian will probably want twin beds. "You'd want us to grow old together and Julian, I have no intentions of growing old."

There are, I'm sure, scads of girls around who would be thrilled to bits to have a relationship with Julian. He does possess certain characteristics which are in demand since we've had this identity revolution, this overlapping of the sexes. Julian is not ashamed to cry. Or at least he tells me he cries and perhaps that is the same thing. I, however, am a traditionalist and like my men hard-boiled. Julian believes in dredging private thoughts out into the open, like all the analysts say is healthy, and he is easy on the eyes. He is intelligent in a well-read, if not good-grasp, sort of way. He has a job and now wants a committed relationship. I would think he'd be quite a grab. "There are lots of girls out there . . ."

"Women," he corrects me.

"Right. Women out there for you. Why would you want me?" I resist the urge to wipe my mouth with my sleeve à la Humphrey Bogart. *I'm nothing but trouble, sweetheart.*

Julian's nebulous devotion is an annoyance, a tickle in my throat. I am too vain a creature to accept that I could be replaced by any number of women. "Don't you see," I raise my voice in displeasure, "it has to be *me* you're wild about. Not some anonymous twat whose billing I fit."

"Shhh," he says. "People are staring."

I wave him off and tell him to go fall in love with one of his students.

He gives me a vexed furrow of the brow and says he couldn't relate to any of them.

"Julian," I ask, "where do you get the idea you could 'relate' to me? You'd be fed up with me inside of two weeks."

Julian tells me this is not so; he'd love me forever and I gag on my mashed potatoes. The thought of eternity with anyone does not stir me but the thought of forever with a whine like Julian is retching. At the very most, I could love Julian for a week or so.

It suddenly dawns on me that perhaps all Julian really wants is to get into my pants. I don't think Julian gets laid a lot. Poor, confused Julian thinks he has to vow to love me forever to get me into bed. But when I tell him all this rigamarole isn't necessary, that I'd have a tumble with him, he gets indignant and accuses me of having a poor self-image, whatever the hell that means.

"How can you think that's all I want from you? Where is your self-esteem?" he wants to know.

"I've got plenty of self-esteem. Aren't you the one who accuses me of having an overflow of self-esteem? Sometimes, all people want from one another is sex."

"Maybe some people. But not me." Julian is so moral. "I want a relationship."

My impatience festers. "Julian, you'd be miserable with me. I run all over town. I'd never be faithful."

Julian leans forward. "Is there someone else?"

I tell him there is always someone else and he wants to know if it is anyone he knows. "Someone we went to school with?" he asks.

"Not someone else specifically. Just that someone else is bound to come along."

"But is there someone now?" Julian asks this as if it matters. When I tell him no, there is no one else at the moment, he appears satisfied and claims to not, then, understand why I can't love him. "As long as there's no one else."

"I can't love you because you tell me you love me and then sit back to see what I'm going to do about it."

"What else am I supposed to do?"

"Everything. I insist upon being wooed." I describe the successful endeavors of past lovers and the means of their pursuit: letters, sonnets, tenacity, perfume, silk stockings, radio dedications. "I'm a pushover for flattery," I tell him.

"You look especially beautiful tonight," he says.

"Shove it, Julian."

Julian cannot fathom why he's pissing me off. He continues to bang his head on the concrete wall asking over and over again what he can do and I keep on telling him that if I have to tell him, the idea behind it is lost.

Julian says, "I used to be wild, you know. I used to have a motorcycle . . . "

"And ride in the fast lane," I finish.

He says he thinks it could work out between us if only I'd give it a chance. I tell him it wouldn't and I won't and to quit nagging — it's not masculine. "I'm only watching out for you," I say. "I'm not the one who would get crushed."

"Don't be so sure," he says with none of the confidence that statement should carry.

The waitress clears away our plates and asks if we want coffee. Julian orders an espresso and I have another beer. He tells me I drink too much.

No matter what he says, his quest for a relationship is high flown in cloudland. He doesn't really want to commit to anyone. "Face it, Julian. If you really wanted a girlfriend, you never would have come to me."

"But I know you better than any other woman.

I'm comfortable with you."

"And how many times do I have to tell you I don't want comfort? I won't have it."

"Then, there's no way?"

"No way, Julian."

He smiles for the first time all evening and says he had a feeling I wouldn't agree to this. And I say, "Maybe if you didn't have that feeling, Julian . . . "

We get the check. Julian turns it over and says, "How much money do you have on you? I don't have enough."

What a washout. I throw a ten spot at him and he asks, "We still can be friends, can't we?"

A Full Life of a Different Nature

Jerking-off is not onomatopoeic for girls the way it is for men. Men get all sorts of names for it. Clever and amusing names. Names that sound like fun. Men get to say they beat meat, flog the dong, stroke the jones, blast the shaft, slap the monkey, climb the flagpole, date Rosey Palm, cast seed, hob the knob, and shoot the load to stone. For me, there aren't so many expressions. Barely a handful and they sound more like embarrassments, or for medicinal purposes, than a rip-roaring good time.

I tell Irving I'm not fazed by the limitations in vocabulary because I've so many options in the act. "Where it counts, Irving."

Irving calls my options "multitudes in the valley of decision." Irving thinks he's a card.

It's not that I don't like sex with men because I do. It's nice. Sometimes, it's very nice but when I engage in sex by myself, I never miss. That's a fact. Even Masters and Johnson say the self-induced orgasm is more intense. They also say masturbating women enjoy many sequential orgasms and that usually physical exhaustion alone terminates an active masturbatory session. In other words, sex with myself is a bonanza.

"So why mess with men at all?" Irving asks and I say, "Because I can't go down on myself, that's why."

Still, the business of jerking-off is a mixed bag. Something like opening Pandora's box and I'm unable to reduce it to the essentials. Oh, to be a pond snail, hermaphroditic and choiceless. However, I don't dare let Irving in on any ambivalence. For Irving, I'm cavalier without conflict. A bawdy libertine who proclaims, without blushing or batting an eye, that I diddle to the tune of Lotus Blossom Queen taking on the Teamsters.

I don't know if Irving buys my bravado or not. Irving's face is impassive. Enigmatic. A Jewish sphinx.

Irving is my analyst. Technically, that's a misnomer but the other words for him are abrasive. Therapist. Shrink. What sort of person looks to be shrunk? "Not me. I'd rather have tits the size of medicine balls and the agility to coil head to tail like a snake. Make me of Amazonian proportions," I say.

"Such a yentzer in the head I never met in my life," Irving says. "Versteche yentzer?" Irving asks do I understand. "A sexual athlete," he translates. "A regular Mickey Mantle of the genitals."

Irving was my husband's suggestion.

Eugene had said, "Maybe you ought to see someone."

At a crowded party I found my husband Eugene necking with a blonde. His eyes were shut. I watched him fumble at her breasts before locking myself in the bathroom. Perched on the edge of the tub, I envisioned sitting in a tufted chair smoking cigarettes watching Eugene and the blonde babe go at it. Humping away while I blew smoke rings. When that picture got dull, I switched channels as if watching television. I put Eugene in the chair, pants around his ankles. The blonde stuck a finger up me, eased me onto the bed. In that version, the blonde had tits the size of medicine balls.

After pulling up my panties, I washed my hands. For form, I flushed the toilet. Then, I got Eugene, taking him by the elbow. "Let's go home, Eugene," I said. "You're drunk. You don't know what you're doing."

The next morning I woke to an apologetic Eugene between my legs. Lifting my head, I peered down and thought, "There's Eugene's face in my pussy." His tongue flicked and kissed and the nicer it felt, the less I connected it to Eugene. There was just some guy eating me out. My head slid back on the pillow as that guy down there began to resemble Mr. Clean of liquid detergent fame. Only my Mr. Clean neither smiled nor winked. Some muscle-bound slave master was toying, sucking and out loud I said, "Hurt me."

"I hurt you?" Eugene popped up. "I'm sorry. I didn't mean to hurt you."

While Eugene showered, I brought back the bald man with the big biceps. I gave him a tattoo of a woman who thrusted when he flexed and because, what the hell, it was my fantasy, I also gave him a twin brother with an eyepatch.

"An eyepatch?" Irving finds this a detail of significance. He coaxes me into remembering that when I was five or six, Captain Hook made me hot. Captain Hook from *Peter Pan*. At that same time, I got a blue plastic record player and a collection of LPs, one of which was sea chanteys. What fortune! Songs that had something to do with Captain Hook. In my bedroom, I took off my clothes and I danced naked to "Blow the Man Down." I gyrated and shimmied for the pirates as they drank rum and sang, "Come all ye young fellows who follow the sea."

I could not get Eugene back in focus. Each time we fucked, I turned him into someone or something else. Anything but Eugene. I had Eugene as grade school principal. Eugene as Chinese emperor, six-inch fingernails scraping at my back. Eugene as low-level Nazi and Eugene as seven men with a Rottweiller.

But even metamorphosized, sex with Eugene left me hanging. Wanting. Panting. For satisfaction, I jerked-off. There was no sign of Eugene then, either. Not so much as a cameo appearance and I was jerking-off a lot. It was becoming somewhat of a hobby. It's what I did in my spare time.

Masturbation is supposed to be a substitute. Something teenage boys and nuns do. Filler. In lieu of a steady bang. Those of us getting regular pooch are not supposed to be fishing around in our own pants. Or are we?

It occurred to me I married a sexual lemon.

It also occurred to me I was a pervert.

"I'm like a shark in a feeding frenzy," I tell Irving. "The more I get laid, the more I jerk-off. It's as if men are foreplay. Do you think I'm a pervert?" I say "pervert" like it's a compliment.

"Nah," Irving says. "A little meshuggeneh, maybe. But not a pervert."

While preparing dinner, I got a sizable cucumber from the refrigerator. Its bulk brought James to mind. James possesses proudly the largest cock imaginable. The first time I saw it, I drew in a deep breath. I understood phallic worship. I wanted to genuflect in its presence.

The cucumber, having it over James in width, wasn't about to slip in on its own. With James, we used sun tan oil. The only lubricant in the kitchen was a tub of garlic butter.

I hoisted myself onto the butcher block counter top. A fantasy featuring James was the obvious choice but I went with Julia Child preparing a feast. I was to be the entree. I coached her androgynous falsetto to instruct, "Coat the cucumber liberally with garlic butter. Now, ease it in gently. Slow-ly. In and out. And in and out. Then, in all the way and Voila! Voila! Voila!"

The cucumber went in the garbage disposal and Eugene came home from work. Sniffing around the kitchen he asked, "Did you make garlic bread? I could swear I smell garlic. What about salad? Did you make salad?"

"No salad," I snapped.

Over dinner I asked Eugene to pass the salt. I asked if his steak were rare enough and was there ever a time when he jerked-off a lot.

Eugene laughed, exposing a mouthful of potatoes in the process. "You bet," he said. "When I was a kid I spent days at a clip pulling my pud over *Playboy* centerfolds, *National Geographic*, the Sears catalogue. Bras and girdles section. Eventually, all the pages would stick together. I'd have to peel them apart. Fifteen-year-old boys rub their dicks raw. Why do you ask?"

"No reason," I said. "Just curious. What about

women? You think women masturbate much?"

"For Christ's sake," Eugene said. "We're eating."

My adventure with the cucumber transformed the Korean vegetable market on my corner into an erotic boutique. Like Pavlov's dog in heat, I couldn't pass by without getting wet. The vegetable bin in my refrigerator was a pleasure dome, bountiful with zucchini, cucumbers, carrots, corn-on-the-cob, and an occasional freak potato. Small radishes acted as bijou balls. Vegetables stay hard for days, weeks. A zucchini never wants a back rub and a carrot couldn't care less if I smoke when we're done.

"But you know what the best part is, Irving? No vegetable ever asks if it was good for me, too."

"You shtup vegetables?" Irving says. "Why not a vibrator or a dildo? What gives with the vegetables?" Irving does, however, concede me on the corn-on-the-cob, nubby-kernelled and mythological.

"My vegetables," I tell Irving indignantly, "are not stand-ins for anything but a battery-operated penis is."

"You'll pardon me," Irving's voice is dry. "I didn't know it made a difference what you stick up yourself had to be of natural fibers."

What I don't tell Irving is that you can't put a vibrator down the garbage disposal. If I couldn't grind up the evidence, I'd be faced with it.

After dinner, Eugene watched TV and I read a newspaper. During a commercial Eugene turned to me and asked, "Maybe you had something garlicky for lunch?"

"You're imagining it," I said and to change the subject read to him from Dear Abby. "Listen to this. A woman writes that during sex with her husband, she has lesbian fantasies. She's concerned. She signed the letter Am I Queer?"

"Why are you reading this to me?" Eugene asked.

"Because it's fascinating. Dear Abby advises her to go with the flow. Any fantasy is perfectly natural. You know, stuff we think is depraved but isn't. Don't you find this fascinating? What do you think Dear Abby fantasizes about?"

And Eugene said, "I think you ought to see someone."

I thought Eugene had meant "see someone" as in "see someone else, have an affair." As I already was seeing someone, I was on the verge of telling him about James when Eugene clarified what he meant by adding, "Someone you can talk to."

For my weekly visits with Irving, I gussy up. Pizazz in gift wrapping. Against the couch of field-mouse brown and orange plaid, I look as out of place here as an anachronism.

Irving has white hair in need of a trim and the chair he sits in is some Scandinavian job advertising his back troubles. Often, Irving speaks to me in Yiddish which I don't much understand but I'm convinced the words are trinkets and baubles spoken to delight me.

In an attempt to give Irving a pearl in return, I tell him a fib. I tell him that in his waiting room, while he was on the phone, I hiked up my skirt and romped. "On that black vinyl chair," I embellish. "It's probably still damp."

"Oy vey," Irving rolls his eyes and I say, "Irving. Relax. Think of it as an offering. Besides, what'd you expect me to do out there? Read *New York* magazine?" I frequently complain about the *New York* magazines in his waiting room to which Irving always says, "You want to read, go to the library."

I grind out my cigarette and suggest to Irving he get leather chairs. "Seriously, Irving. Vinyl is tacky."

Next to the ashtray is a box of Kleenex. Also on the glass coffee table is a bowl of fruit. Two tangerines, some plums, and a banana which Irving avoids when we discuss my affinity for plant life.

I met Violet for lunch in a restaurant that could've been a hothouse, all glass and greenery. Violet and I claim to have no secrets from the other. But we do. Violet knows about James but not the scoop on his cock. And while I did tell her I found Eugene necking with a blonde, I omitted that I went to the bathroom to jerk-off over it. All I'd said to Violet was, "He should've had the decency to do it behind my back." Nor does Violet have any idea that I turn Eugene into an assortment of things ranging from a coven of cloven-footed warlocks to a rutabaga.

In college Violet talked me into peeing with her against a tree. She said it was that which made boys such close friends. How boys achieve a camaraderie rare in women. "Men claim it's the army or the locker room," Violet had said. "But that's not so. It's peeing together on trees."

Not that Violet always knows of what she speaks. Violet thinks Irving is a quack. She says no reasonable therapist quotes scripture at you. She also says Irving is trying to seduce me.

Over lunch I asked Violet to pass the salt. I asked how was the chicken salad and did she masturbate much. Violet turned puce. I was embarrassing her. "What kind of question is that?" she asked.

"Aren't we best friends?" I put on a hurt look. "I thought we had no secrets. Boys discuss jerking-off constantly. They even do it in front of each other. No wonder men have strong friendships. Women get so prissy over the same subject."

I'd successfully bullied Violet into spilling the dirt about her weekend in Vermont with someone called Walter. Expecting romance, Violet dolled up in a silk chemise but Walter's underwear had holes in it. "And it was stained," Violet shuddered. "You'd think he'd have sprung for a new pair for the occasion. And if that weren't wretched enough," Violet said, "we had to watch John Wayne movies on TV. Did you ever notice that all men who are clods in bed just happen to be big John Wayne fans?"

"Do you like John Wayne?" I ask Irving.

"Who?" Irving says. "Who's John Wayne? Oh, you mean the cowboy? Nah. Such chozzerai."

"We had sex twice," Violet said. "It was lousy sex. I could not get past that underwear. During the drive home, I wanted to nap so I got into the back seat and I did it. You know, what you asked about. In the back seat of Walter's Volvo on I-95. When I came," Violet said, "I cried."

"You cried? Why?"

"I don't know. The whole thing seemed so pathetic. The only good sex I had the entire weekend and I had it alone."

"Do you ever cry after you masturbate?" Irving asks.

"No," I say. "Never."

It's true I don't shed tears but there are moments of melancholy, heavy with grief. Post coital tristesse without the coital and the desire to weep fades the way a dream does. To admit this to Irving would, however, put a crimp in my style so what I say is, "No. I don't cry

141

but sometimes I think I've blown a hole through the mattress."

"What about you?" Violet asked. "Do you do it? You know, masturbate?"

"No," I said. "Never. I asked you because Irving had asked me and he was surprised that I didn't so I was curious."

"Hmmph, Irving," Violet snorted and I lost the opportunity to discover what Violet fantasized about in the back seat of Walter's Volvo.

There's a practical joke I'd heard of where a group of boys propose to the new kid on the block that they all sit in a circle, lights out, and jerk-off. Of course, none do more than unzip their flies and make the appropriate noises. Only the new kid really goes for it. When his seed is cast, he finds himself in the spotlight, spent pud in hand and jizz on the floor.

I treated Violet to lunch because I felt like a bit of a heel. As if I'd played a practical joke on her.

In a kitschy shop in SoHo, the dressing rooms were salvaged confessional booths revamped with mirrors but otherwise intact. Harmless heresy, I thought, as I closed the curtain and stripped to my underwear. Black bra. Black garter belt. In a confessional. Come hither cheek peeking out from pink panties. In a confessional. With one hand, I went in search of rapture. But suppose some saleswoman on commission burst in to zip me up, to insist the red dress was made for me? She'd find me jerking-off in a dressing room that had once been a confessional. She'd think I was a pervert and call Security. As if burned, my hand snapped back. I punked out and left the red dress on the hanger.

"Now it's a dressing room," I explain the layout to Irving. "But it used to be a real confessional. With a priest on the other side. A faceless priest."

"And this excited you?" Irving asks. "You were aroused?"

"I couldn't resist, Irving. I dropped to the floor. Legs spread. Knees bent. Oh, rapture. Oh, bliss. Brazen hussy." I perjure myself in analysis which isn't really analysis. Might as well throw in some hosannas while I'm at it.

Irving makes a note on his pad like he's Saint Peter at the gate or Santa Claus checking his list.

Before coming to Irving's office I jerked-off but didn't wash my hands. As a token of affection. Or, to prove something. If Irving knows this, he doesn't let on. What he does ask is if I'm familiar with the story of Lilith.

"Lilith was the first woman," Irving says. "Before Eve. She was also made from clay. As Adam was. Therefore, when Adam requested Lilith lie on the ground so he could mount her, she very nicely told Adam he could get down on the dirt himself, thank you very much. Not that Lilith wasn't interested in fooling around," Irving footnotes. "She just didn't fancy the missionary position. Well, Adam insisted and still, Lilith refused. Finally, furious, she uttered magic words which lifted her into the air. Off she went, leaving Adam without a girlfriend. So, in stepped God who dispatched some angels to find Lilith and bring her back to Adam." Irving stops and folds his hands as if that were the end of the story.

"Well," I want to know. "Did the angels find her?"

"Oh yes," Irving says. "The angels found Lilith by the Red Sea where she was cavorting with demons and devils."

I make mention that the Red Sea sounds like the predecessor of Club Med and Irving says, "Exactly. And Lilith knew as much, too, because she asked the angels how, after all this, could they expect her to return to Adam and live like a housewife. It's not possible. And that's when God made Eve."

"But what happened to Lilith?" I ask.

"It's not important," Irving says. "Let it suffice to say Lilith had a full life of a different nature."

I wanted James to fuck me with his saxophone. James is a musician plus a waiter. I'd been married eight months when I took up with him. James is rather lean minded. He thinks that big cock of his is the cat's meow. This is one way James reveals he's a chuckle-head. It is an impressive cock but regardless, sex with

James must be choreographed. As if getting him from the Lower East Side to the Lincoln Tunnel I direct, "More. There. No, here. To the left. Lower. Harder. Deeper." But the really miserable part is no sooner do I say, "Yes. Yes, that's it," does James slip. Then he asks, "Was it good for you, too?"

Irving calls James "the boyfriend" which sounds silly to me. But there's no real word for what James is. Lover is one of those words that gives me the creeps, a point Irving finds curious but I don't. James is very pretty and constantly broke. Paramour is the word I use for James. Paramour I like. Love on the side. Come to think of it, Eugene is also love on the side. "Only I am the main event," I say.

To back up that claim, I describe for Irving my latest fantasy. It has to do with people giving me objects. Things I make disappear. It's like audience participation in a magic act.

James did not take seriously my request for his saxophone. "Yeah, I'll fuck you with my horn, baby." He waved his cock around as if it were funny.

In a secluded corner in Central Park, six blocks from Irving's office, James pulled clumps of grass from the ground and asked what my sex life with Eugene was like.

"I never think about Eugene in connection with sex," I said. "When Eugene and I fuck, I think of other

145

things."

"What about us?" James wanted to know. "When we fuck, do you think about me?"

"I think about your saxophone."

James took the truth as a big joke.

"When fucking James, I think about his cock. Only it's not attached to him but it's free floating like a winged cherub. Other times, I imagine I'm with a vegetable. In place of James."

"Any vegetable?" Irving inquires. "Or a specific one?"

"A head of cabbage," I grin. "Otherwise, it's his saxophone I'm after."

In Central Park, six blocks from Irving's office, I gave James five dollars to get us something to drink.

"No problem," said James. "I'll be right back."

I told him to take his time but knew he wouldn't. Before I could even get a fantasy rolling, James returned with two cans of Pepsi. "Miss me?" he asked.

Looking off in the direction of Irving's office I said, "Terribly."

"I've quit having fantasies," I announce.

"Impossible," Irving says. "You shut your eyes, you must think of something."

"The fact is, Irving, I don't shut my eyes. I keep them open to watch myself in the mirror. I'm an incredible turn-on. My flesh. My breasts. My thighs. My fingers. My toenails painted red like rosebuds."

"Ah," Irving says. "Your eyes shall be opened and ye shall be as gods."

"Yeah," I say. "That's it. I'm the star in my own blue movie."

I tried telling James about how I jerk-off. Actually, I'd wanted to give him a demonstration like a vacuum cleaner salesman. In his bed, while he ate chocolate ice cream from the container, I asked if he masturbates much. James did not like the question. "I have you," he said. "Why should I masturbate?"

"But you don't have me. Not completely."

James took that as a reference to my being married and said, "But you don't even think about him."

"I'd like to watch you jerk-off." I told a bold-faced lie. I had no interest in watching James jerk-off but I did have an itch for him to watch me. I'd have watched him for equal play. Tit for tat.

Busy spooning more ice cream into his mouth, James didn't respond so I ventured on. "If you show me," I dared, "I'll show you."

"I don't want to watch you masturbate." James' lower lip was rimmed with chocolate. "That's dykey. I want to come inside you."

"Such opportunity," Irving comments, "and the

boyfriend shrugs it off. He's a bit of a shlemiel, this boyfriend?"

"More than a bit," I concur despite an uncertainty of the definition. "In a way, I feel sorry for him," I tell Irving. "He's no idea what's been lost. If James had bowed at my feet, I'd never have left his bed. I'd have given him all my money and worldly goods. If James had only watched me jerk-off, we would've found faith. The sort of faith granted from having witnessed a miracle."

"And which miracle did you have in mind?" Irving asks. "The burning bush but the bush is not consumed?"

Violet thinks Irving's aim is to seduce me because Violet gets the facts in fractions. Only Irving is given the whole pie. Or, almost the whole pie. Or, more than the whole pie. I have no shame before Irving but I do have pride. I'm like the girl who confesses, "Forgive me, Father, for I have sinned. I had impure thoughts" but neglects to mention that he, stripped of cassock, votive candle in hand, was the object of the impure thoughts. Or, I'm the girl who fabricates sin. Marvelous transgressions worthy of Boschian panels. To get the priest to sit up, take notice, I bring pizazz to the chore of forgiving petty human failings.

Eugene is also after me to give Irving up but for different reasons. "It's getting expensive," he said.

I called Eugene a shnorrer but he doesn't know

Yiddish at all. "That's another thing," he said. "You're drifting away from me. Like sometimes you're not there."

"I know what you mean," I told him. "Sometimes, it's like you're not there, either."

"It's that I'm such a sex tomato," I say to Irving. "A lust puppy. I need my equal to satisfy me and to date, I'm the only one qualified for the job."

Irving asks what I plan to do then and I shrug. "Have another affair. Try my luck with a different one."

Irving tells me King Solomon had seven hundred wives and three hundred concubines but it's unclear as to what he's driving at. I wait for a hint but he's not giving one. I'd never want to get into a poker game with Irving.

"Are you telling me to have a thousand affairs?" I ask. "That salvation is in numbers?"

"No," Irving says. "I'm telling you his wives turned away his heart."

"Big deal. He still had the harem, right?"

"Big deal?" One of Irving's fuzzy eyebrows goes up. "Big deal. The sex tomato-lust puppy says big deal. Big deal to love. Is that it, sex tomato? Tell me, Miss Sex Tomato-Lust Puppy, have you got a nerve ending or two someplace besides the erogenous zones?"

I've never seen Irving angry before. He doesn't shout or bang his fist but it's the even toned ominous fury of the Jewish God, the sort of anger that lets you think you're in deep trouble. "What are you going to do?" I ask. "Banish me?"

"'Too easy," Irving waves that off. "You're going to get down to geshefte," and I wonder if that means down on my knees when Irving says in English, "Business. Quit the jerking-off here."

"What do you mean quit?"

"Here in my office where you masturbate without your hands. Where you put on your Jezebel costumes and brag. That jerking-off." Irving leans forward out of his Scandinavian chair and sweetly now, as if concerned something will break, he says, "I don't buy the bravado."

I feel as if Irving has invaded something private. I feel exposed and I want to cover up only I don't know which parts are involved. Instead, I reach into the fruit bowl and choose a plum. I hold it in my hand, not sure what to do next until Irving tells me, "Go ahead. Eat, darling. Eat."